WILLERBY MANOR

Recent Titles by Aileen Armitage from Severn House

ANNABELLA

CAMBERMERE

A DOUBLE SACRIFICE

FLAMES OF FORTUNE

JASON'S DOMINION

MALLORY KEEP

A PASSIONATE CAUSE

THE RADLEY CURSE

A THEFT OF HONOUR

THE SEAMSTRESS

A WINTER SERPENT

WILLERBY MANOR

Aileen Armitage

This title first published in Great Britain 2002 by
SEVERN HOUSE PUBLISHERS LTD of
9–15 High Street, Sutton, Surrey SM1 1DF.
First published in 1973 in paperback format only in the USA
under the title *A Scent of Violets* and pseudonym of *Ruth Fabian*.
This title first published in the USA 2003 by
SEVERN HOUSE PUBLISHERS INC of
595 Madison Avenue, New York, N.Y. 10022.

British Library Cataloguing in Publication Data

Armitage, Aileen, 1930–
   Willerby Manor
   1. Kidnapping victims - Fiction
   2. Historical fiction
   I. Title
   823.9'14 [F]

   ISBN 0-7278-5899-8

20090306

Except where actual historical events and characters are being
described for the storyline of this novel, all situations in this
publication are fictitious and any resemblance to living persons
is purely coincidental.

Printed and bound in Great Britain by
MPG Books Ltd., Bodmin, Cornwall.

ONE

The tiled corridors of Madame Roland's Academy for Young Ladies rang to the sound of scurrying footsteps and girlish giggles. Linnet Grey stood at the head of the staircase and tried to hush the noise.

"Miss Rebecca, Miss Susannah, please! You know Madame insists that going to bed must be accompanied by silence! If she hears you, she will be angry."

"Madame! She is always angry! There is no pleasing her!" Rebecca chuckled as she swept by. But the noise was subdued to a rustle of skirts and a hissing of gaslamps as the door to a chamber downstairs opened and Madame's voice was heard, loud and dominating.

"Miss Grey! I distinctly hear sounds! You are not doing your work effectively. I shall speak to you later."

Footsteps retreated and the door slammed. Linnet sighed. Interviews with Madame were never pleasant, and more especially since Linnet was now no longer a pupil but a pupil-teacher in the establishment. Since her parents' sudden death a year ago Madame had allowed her to remain here in a working capacity, but she obviously regarded herself as a benefactress, a doler-out of charity to Linnet, for she spared no effort to make her life as difficult as she could.

Linnet followed the girls into the dormitory to see them safely settled down for the night. The smaller girls needed help to get out of their chemises and drawers quickly if they were to be in their nightdresses before Madame rang the bell for lights out. Madame did not believe in an unnecessary waste of gas.

When she paused at last, flushed from her efforts, Linnet saw Susannah sitting on Rebecca's bed and looking at a piece of paper and giggling. Rebecca snatched the paper and pushed it under the bedclothes when she saw Linnet looking at them.

"What have you there?" Linnet asked, going towards them.

"Nothing." Rebecca's face went pink.

"Then what are you two whispering about?"

"My father took me to the theatre tonight," Rebecca replied, "and I wanted to tell Susannah all about it."

"I see."

"I was telling her about the marvellous actress, Chantal Legris, and how my father took me to have supper at the restaurant afterwards, and . . ."

A loud bell cut short Rebecca's enthusiastic, breathless account of the evening's adventure. Linnet smiled.

"There—now you'll have to finish undressing in the dark." She turned off all the gas lamps in the dormitory, bade the girls good night and withdrew. Madame was waiting outside the door.

"Come downstairs," she said with some asperity, and turned and led the way. Linnet followed with resignation, knowing the rebuke that was to follow. And it did. In the vestibule Madame could contain her anger no longer. She made no bones about intimating her dissatisfaction with Linnet's work, admitting begrudgingly that she taught moderately well within the classroom, but decrying Linnet's almost total lack of discipline.

"Why, even now upstairs I heard you indulging in conversation with some of them, at bedtime too, when you know I insist on absolute silence! How can one expect the girls to conform to rules if you do not?"

Linnet hung her head and listened with clasped hands, knowing better than to answer Madame's rhetorical question. Madame fumed on, coming at last to the point Linnet was dreading. Perhaps, she said, it would be better if Linnet were to discard the idea of teaching and seek employment elsewhere.

"After all," said Madame, spreading her hands, "this is not a charitable institution, and the thirty pounds a year I am paying you could perhaps more profitably be spent on a better-qualified teacher who would do my bidding. You had better think it over, Miss Grey. I have no more time to waste now—there is a visitor awaiting me in my study."

Madame swept off haughtily into her study, and Linnet could hear her voice murmuring honeyed words of apology to the guest before she closed the door. Linnet turned and crossed the flagstoned floor to the stairs thoughtfully. She was reluctant to join the other teachers in the common-room, vying to seize the chairs nearest the tiny coal fire which was all the ration Madame would permit for the evening. And in all this echoing building there was no other warm spot to go, save to her own bed in the dormitory. She decided perhaps it would be best to go to bed.

She climbed the stairs and walked along the cold, tiled corridor to the dormitory. She shivered. Indeed, bed was by far the most comfortable place to be on a wintry night like this. She would be glad to be warmly tucked abed in her woollen nightgown.

The dormitory was dark and silent. All the girls appeared to be already fast asleep as Linnet passed by on tiptoe the twelve little beds to her own curtained recess at the far end of the room. Near Rebecca's bed she paused. The curtain was not fully drawn across the window and a shaft of moonlight fell across the bare floorboards. As Linnet rounded the bed carefully to adjust the curtain, she saw a piece of paper on the floor alongside the bed, and stooped automatically to pick it up. Madame waged a constant war on litter, and nothing infuriated her more than odd scraps of paper lying about. Linnet pocketed the paper to dispose of it later, drew the curtains noiselessly so that the moonlight was blocked out, and tiptoed to her own bed.

Once behind her curtain, Linnet deliberated whether to light the candle and wash in the cold water in the ewer, or to undress in the dark and get

10

into bed quickly. It was bitterly cold, so she decided on the latter. Her bare feet almost froze on the floor before she was finally undressed and climbed into her nightgown. She snuggled between the blankets gratefully and clasped her feet with her hands until the circulation returned.

She sighed heavily as she recalled the evening's encounter with Madame Roland. She had not intended to offend her, but somehow it seemed as though she could never please her employer however hard she tried. Linnet found the girls friendly and pleasant, and liked to chat with them briefly when the opportunity occurred, but Madame was ever harsh to any of her teachers whom she found being friendly with the pupils. It was bad for discipline, she said. Maintaining an aloof and icy manner was the only way to ensure instant obedience, but Linnet found it impossible to remain icily aloof. She wanted and needed the friendship of the girls, some of them only a year or so younger than herself. After all, she had no friends or even family of her own to turn to for warmth, and the smiles and confidences of her pupils meant much to her.

What would she do if Madame were indeed to find her unsatisfactory and dismiss her, as she threatened? Linnet had no training for any other position, and to earn a living somehow was vital, now that her parents were dead. Linnet tried to recall a vision of her mother's face, but found it hazy and fleeting. After all, she had never really known her mother very well, and her father scarcely at all.

11

Linnet tried to remember her early years, living in a little house in London with her mother while her father was away at sea. Her tall, bearded, hearty father had loved his sea-going life and his fine ship, the *Linnet*, and had been proud to name his only child after his beloved ship. Whenever he came home he burst into the house like a gale, bringing laughter and life with him and a radiant smile to her mother's face, only to leave again very soon, leaving behind a haze of tobacco smoke and a sad-faced wife waving from behind the lace curtain.

Mother had not seemed to exist while he was away. She glided quietly about the house like a ghost, a wistful, far-away look on her pale face. She had answered dutifully when Linnet spoke to her, but her mind was not on her words. Linnet knew she was pining for her husband, and not even her child could make up for his prolonged absences.

Then one day Father had asked Mother to give up the little house and come away to sea with him, accompanying him on his voyages to the farthest corners of the earth. He explained regretfully that it was no life for a child, however, and Linnet should be placed in a boarding school. Mother had agreed eagerly, overjoyed at not having to be parted from him again, and Linnet had found herself, at the age of twelve, placed at Madame Roland's Academy for Young Ladies, and her parents no more than fleeting visitors once every couple of years.

Until last year, that was. And then one sultry summer evening Madame called Linnet to her study, and

Linnet had gone with trembling heart, wondering what transgression she had committed, what exercise had displeased Madame, or what error of dress or deportment. But Madame had eyed her thoughtfully for some time, letting her lorgnette fall unnoticed from her eye, before placing her large, capable hands on Linnet's shoulders and revealing to her sadly that a sudden storm on the China seas had made Linnet an orphan.

Madame had been kind, in her way. She had been quick to reassure Linnet that there was no cause for worry over finances. As Linnet was now a senior girl and reasonably competent, Madame would offer her a post as a pupil-teacher, subject to satisfactory work, and so it had been for the past year or more. Only now Madame was showing more than a hint of irritation over Linnet's work, and before long Linnet feared she would carry out her threat of dismissal.

Linnet felt very dispirited. Where could she go if she were to leave here? She lay awake half the night worrying over her future. Before dawn, unable to sleep, she rose and washed and dressed by candlelight. She might as well be up early, ready to help the children dress, for it would soon be time for the rising bell.

As she smoothed down the skirt of her dark merino dress she felt crackling in the pocket and withdrew from it a piece of paper. It was the paper she had picked up by moonlight last night. Linnet bent closer to the candle to examine it.

Words proclaiming a new play at a London theatre

13

blazed forth from the folded sheet, but Linnet had eyes only for the picture of a lovely girl beneath, her proud head tilted high, aware of her beauty and vitality. Beneath the picture the caption read, "Chantal Legris, the leading lady".

Linnet sighed and could barely resist a tinge of envy. How little she had in common with Chantal Legris. Linnet was orphaned and unloved, working hard for a living of which she might be robbed at any moment, while Chantal was the toast of London, mobbed by admirers and pursued, no doubt, by half the eligible bachelors of the city, all anxious to shower her with gifts and compliments, while at home her proud parents probably placed her portrait at dead centre of their mantelpiece, and listened with glowing pride to visitors' rapturous comments.

The rising bell cut short Linnet's envious surmisings. She lit a taper from her candle and lit the gas lamps, murmuring encouraging exhortations to her charges to rise and dress as she did so. She extinguished the taper when the last lamp hissed and spluttered into life and crossed to Rebecca's bed and shook her sleeping shoulder.

"Miss Rebecca, time to get up," she admonished, then added as Rebecca sat up and rubbed her eyes, "And I think this is yours, is it not?"

She held out the theatre programme. Rebecca took it eagerly and thanked Linnet as she folded it and put it away in her locker. As Linnet saw the face of Chantal Legris being creased and folded, a sudden fierce desire rose inside her. She wanted to see this lovely, legendary creature for herself. And why not?

she thought defiantly. She could go to the Alhambra to see the star if only Madame would grant her a free evening. And life was so fraught with anxieties that she deserved some diversion. Yes, that was what she would do, if only the opportunity occurred.

TWO

All day Linnet nursed the small seed of determination to go to the theatre and see Chantal Legris. She longed for Madame to pronounce that it was time for Linnet to have an evening off duty, for such a concession was not a regular event in Madame's regime.

Contemplating the outing gave rise to a feeling of daredevil excitement, for Linnet was well aware that even in these enlightened days of 1882 ladies did not normally go to the theatre unaccompanied. Madame would arch her eyebrows in scornful disgust if she knew what her pupil-teacher proposed, but Linnet would not tell her. Life was so uneventful that she had need of the stimulus of an exciting adventure. Decorous or not, she would slip away to the theatre just so soon as the chance presented itself.

But when the opportunity came, it did not bring with it the exhilaration that Linnet had expected. She was sitting at her high iron desk surveying the rows of well-scrubbed, shining faces with neatly plaited hair listening to her attentively, when the door of the classroom opened. The girls leapt politely to their feet as Madame swept in and approached the dais where

Linnet sat. Linnet too rose and stepped down from the dais.

"Miss Grey, a word with you in private," said Madame curtly, and turned and led the way out into the corridor. Linnet followed obediently, aware of the low hum of conversation that began in the classroom the moment she closed the door. Madame would hear and complain, she thought, but Madame's mind was obviously on other matters.

"Miss Grey, I should be glad of your absence from the Academy this afternoon and evening," she said abruptly, taking her lorgnette from her eye and polishing it vigorously with a lace handkerchief as she spoke. Linnet gazed at her in surprise, but knew better than to question her employer's reason. Madame apparently considered while she polished, how to choose her words with care.

"I am to have a visitor this afternoon, a young lady, a former governess whose employers are leaving the country. I wish to interview her and then put her to test in the classroom to see how she can cope with thirty girls instead of just two." Madame replaced her lorgnette and regarded Linnet haughtily. "I propose to give her your class, Miss Grey, to put her through her paces. They are a set of lively girls who will test her abilities. Therefore I would prefer you to be absent on the occasion, you understand?"

Linnet nodded. She wondered if Madame was being unusually considerate towards the prospective new teacher, relieving her of the embarrassment of having to tackle Linnet's class under Linnet's observation, or whether Madame was in fact proposing to test out the new teacher with a view to replacing Linnet. If the new woman were given Linnet's class permanently then Madame would have no further use for Linnet's services and the path to her dismissal would be clear.

"So you may absent yourself after lunch for the rest of the day," Madame Roland concluded. Linnet returned to her class and busied herself recapturing the girls' lost attention until the bell clanged for lunchtime, and as the girls hastened away, chattering and excited, Linnet gathered her books and went upstairs to the dormitory. Her apprehension over the new teacher's visit was tempered by the exciting thought that tonight she would be free to go to the theatre.

After lunch, which was a scanty but nourishing affair, with more time given over to correcting the girls' manners and hushing their raised voices than to eating, Linnet went back to her recess. What should she do with the afternoon? There were no friends she could visit, and drizzling rain made walking in the park an unenviable prospect. Still, she consoled herself, since she had so little money in her reticule, she could save the cab fare by walking the fairly long distance to London's West End, look in the shop windows and then have a cup of refreshing tea before going to the theatre. Yes, that was what she would do.

Her one good dress was the dark grey merino one with the slight bustle she was wearing. It had consumed quite a large portion of Linnet's meagre salary, but at the time she had considered it a good investment to have one good frock as befitted her new position as a teacher. And her hat, too. A modest enough affair, but a respectable addition to her wardrobe with its decorous half-veil and its minute bunch of cherries. That, worn with her warm, serviceable black ulster, should render her both warm and comfortable enough for the long walk to the theatre.

Linnet brushed both her dress and her cloth boots meticulously before putting on her ulster and hat. She made sure her reticule contained her small amount of money, a handkerchief and smelling-salts in case the theatre was stuffy, and then drew on her black gloves. At last she was ready. At the front door she paused and sniffed the damp air outside. It was exciting to be leaving the safety of the Academy and going up-town on an adventure, to catch a glimpse of a woman whose way of life was so vastly different from her own.

The rain held off during Linnet's long walk through the cobbled streets, but as she neared the area where the theatre lay, the drizzle began again, steady and persistent. Linnet had planned to visit the shops, but the steady rain made the idea of window-shopping impracticable. She would be soaked long before going to the play tonight.

As she walked along the street in search of a modest-looking tea-room where she could rest for a while, Linnet remembered the reason for her unexpected freedom and wondered how the woman on probation in her classroom was faring. Would Linnet find on her return to the Academy tonight that the stranger had been appointed and Madame was waiting only for Linnet to pack her bag before she put the new woman in charge of her class and dormitory? Linnet brushed the problem firmly from her mind. Tonight she would enjoy the show first and face the possible problem later.

She drank her tea from an earthenware pot in a quiet, unassuming little café in a side street, then sat and watched the other customers until the clock on the wall showed that it would soon be time for the evening performance to begin. She would set off now and take her time in reaching the theatre.

London's streets were busy now with people setting off in search of an evening's diversion. It was no longer raining but the pavements were still wet, and as the lamplighter went on his rounds the cobblestones took on a dull gleam under their hissing lights. Hansom cabs plied the streets and Linnet found it difficult to make her way along the crowded pavements, but when at last she reached Leicester Square there was still a quarter of an hour to go before the show began.

Small knots of people were beginning to gather about the theatre entrance. Linnet's heart began to flutter in embarrassment. So far as she could see, she was the only unescorted woman in sight. Perhaps she had been a little rash, after all, in her impetuous decision to come here.

A forlorn-looking old woman sat on an upturned box under a lamp, a basket of violets in her ample lap. She looked up eagerly at Linnet's approach.

"Violets, lady? Lovely bunch of violets," she croaked hopefully. Linnet felt a surge of pity for the poor old creature, sitting huddled and dejected out of doors on such a night. On a sudden impulse she opened her reticule and drew out a coin.

The old woman's flaccid face broke into a smile and she selected the least limp of her violets to hand to her young customer. Linnet fastened the sweet-scented bunch to her lapel, then bade the old woman good evening before going on.

Outside the theatre she paused. A tall, dark, clean-shaven man was barring her way and Linnet stepped aside to allow him to pass.

He did not pass, but stood there facing her. Linnet could not help but notice his dark, piercing gaze before she made to pass him, but he stepped in front of her again.

"Will you come home with me?"

Linnet was startled, both by his low, vibrant voice, deep and compelling, and by the question. "I beg your pardon?" she said. She could not believe her ears.

"I asked you to come home with me—now. Will you come?"

Linnet was astounded. She had heard aright after all. What was the matter with the fellow? Was he crazy? He looked sane enough, handsome even, in a cold, reserved way, but his gaze was very intense. She shifted uncomfortably, and then another thought struck her. He was well-dressed, in evening wear and with a cape—was he perhaps a wealthy dandy in search of an evening's fun and had mistaken her for . . . Oh, no! He surely could not have taken her for a prostitute! Linnet's cheeks flushed hotly at the thought.

"Excuse me," she said coolly, and made to push past his broad frame to the theatre door, but he took hold of her arm. Linnet flared at him. "Let me go, sir, this instant, or I shall scream for help," she said firmly, and felt his hold loosen. There were people all about them and he could hardly attempt to drag her away unnoticed.

His hand dropped. Linnet thrust forward towards the door amongst the press of people, and inside the foyer she looked about her before fumbling in her purse for her money. He was nowhere to be seen. Thank heaven!

Linnet felt shaken and flustered for a moment by the strange way he had accosted her, and not a little concerned. Surely there was nothing about her dress or behaviour that suggested she was a loose woman, was there? Why else should a strange man invite her home with him, and so brusquely too? Was it because she was a woman alone? And then, did men usually take their casual women acquaintances home with them? From Linnet's limited knowledge, she had always understood that such women had an establishment of their own where they took their clients. It was odd, very odd, but not serious enough to upset herself over, or to warrant calling the police. In any event, the show was about to begin.

Linnet craned over from her seat high in the gods to watch the lovely Chantal far below. And the actress proved how she merited the status of a star, for her acting was incredibly professional and her singing wrung tears from the audience. The wistful, plaintive creature twisting the hearts of her audience entranced

25

Linnet. It was like watching a beautiful, cultured, graceful angel moving and speaking there below. And there was something more. There was something indefinably familiar about the lovely face and glowing red hair of the girl who was the focus of all eyes. Linnet could not place what it was, for from such a high vantage point, close to the ceiling of the vast auditorium, the face of the entrancing creature down below was indistinct, but fascinating nonetheless.

As the show neared its end, Linnet longed again to have a closer view of this clever woman, a last glimpse of a fairy-tale creature she would probably never see again.

As the orchestra gathered momentum for its last great, glorious burst in the finale, Linnet crept from her seat and down the many flights of stairs and outside. She would go round to the stage door and there, with luck, she might gain a final close glimpse of Chantal as she emerged. It was only a possibility, she knew, for the doorway might be blocked by admirers and stage-door johnnies, or Chantal might stay behind in her dressing-room for supper after the show. But it was worth trying.

The stage door stood ajar, a single gas lamp spluttering above it. No one else was about and Linnet stood on the step and hesitated whether to wait outside in the drizzle, or to go just within the door and wait there. The clop-clop of hoofbeats echoed through the deserted street, then stopped at the corner. A man descended from the cab and strode towards her. As he walked within the arc of lamplight

26

Linnet recognised with a start the strange, abrupt man who had accosted her earlier. He stopped before her, his feet astride and his hands jutting on his hips beneath his cloak.

"Well?" he demanded. The voice was still low, but its tone was peremptory.

Linnet's heart fluttered. Should she answer him or dart inside the door and slam it? He came a step closer.

"Will you come?"

Linnet felt terror rising in her. "No!" she cried.

"Very well. Otto!" He raised his voice on the last word and Linnet heard soft footsteps padding towards her in the darkness. The next thing she knew something heavy and warm was thrown over her head, and she was suffocated in thick folds of woollen cloth and there was an overpowering smell of something that was sickly-sweet. She tried in vain to cry out, for the thick stuff found its way into her mouth every time she opened it, and the sweet smell made her senses reel. Then strong arms engulfed her and propelled her along the street.

Linnet was terrified, for however she gasped and choked she could not draw breath. She wanted to beg her assailant for mercy, but her lungs could not grasp the air they needed. Her knees began to sag. Oh, God, have mercy! She prayed inwardly. A cab door slammed.

A voice barked sharply. "Take Miss Grey down to Willerby, Otto, and take good care she does not escape."

Linnet dimly recognised the voice of the man at the stage door and that was her last conscious thought before she sank into oblivion. As the coach clattered away into the night, a limp bunch of violets lay unheeded on the wet pavement outside the stage door.

THREE

What seemed like hours later to Linnet she felt herself being forced back into slowly-returning consciousness. It was like fighting one's way through a long dark tunnel, to the accompaniment of strange rattling and rumbling sounds.

At last she came to. She was lying back on the seat of a coach, but it was no ordinary hansom cab, for the seats were spacious and luxuriously upholstered and there were little brocade head-cushions above the seats facing her. And a man. A huge, beefy, broad-shouldered man of middle age, sitting hunched forward in his dark brown greatcoat and watching her closely.

Linnet made no move while her brain was beginning to function again. The man's black eyes glowed alertly under his bushy dark brows, and he sat with the tense air of an animal about to spring. Linnet began to remember. The man at the stage door—his call to Otto—and the smothering, choking that followed. She breathed deeply, gratified to be able to fill her lungs freely again.

The man did not move, but the carraige clattered noisily on over the cobblestones and every now and again Linnet could hear the crack of a whip. She glanced at the windows, but there were blinds drawn on every one and she could see nothing. The whole scene had a strange air of unreality—the motionless, wary man and the luxurious seats, the silence and the hurtling of the carriage through the night. Was it really happening, she wondered, or was it all a dream and very soon the rising bell would recall her to the dormitory and the bustle of a new day's work? The strange, silent, bowler-hatted man opposite was undoubtedly a figment of her overwrought imagination, she thought confusedly, as she struggle to sit upright, but the huge, hairy hand that reached out to restrain her was no trick of imagination. His grip was hard and hurtful on her arm.

Linnet blinked at him and struggled to collect her wits. His bushy eyebrows met in an angry frown, as if willing her to be silent and be still. He was real enough. Linnet's first thought then was to scream for help, but his fierce expression seemed to indicate that he had anticipated the thought, for the grip on her arm tightened. Linnet winced. She decided not to scream—not yet, anyway for the brute might attack her.

After a moment his hold relaxed slightly and, as Linnet made to sit back, he grew less suspicious and finally let her arm go. But he still sat tensed on the edge of his seat, alert and ready. Linnet forced herself to appear calm and sat back in her seat as if this were any ordinary hansom-cab ride.

Strange that he had not spoken, she thought. If he

were in league with the man outside the theatre, then he must be Otto, the name the man had called out into the night. What were his orders? To conduct her to some discreet London house where the gentleman would follow at a safe distance? Linnet grew angry. If the gentleman thought she would play the willing harlot, he had a surprise in store. Her refusal to accompany him could not have been more emphatic.

And what an odd way to capture a victim to seduce! Abduction, that was the word for it—sheer physical strength to force her to go with him. And what a coward he was, to employ a brute like Otto to do his dirty work for him!

What was it she heard the man say before she fainted? Linnet tried hard to recollect. Willerby—that was it. Otto was to take her to Willerby. But where on earth was that? Linnet could not remember having heard of any London suburb of that name. Perhaps it was the name of a house. But wherever it was, she would devise some means of eluding Otto before they reached there.

Linnet's stomach muscles began to lose their tension and she felt less frightened. Otto seemed to believe she would cause him no trouble now, for he too had sat back into his seat, though his dark eyes never left her face. Perhaps if she acted docile long enough she could catch him off-guard and leap for the door. But she must bide her moment, for the carriage was travelling at high speed.

Then suddenly a niggling memory of something slipped into her mind and instantly out again. What was it? She worried and ferreted at the elusive thought. Something the man had said—something as she was just losing consciousness.

Then suddenly it came. Miss Grey, he had said; take Miss Grey down to Willerby. He had known who she was! It was no casual picking up of an attractive-looking girl in the street, after all. He had kown her and wanted her to come with him for some specific reason!

But if his aim was not seduction but some other legitimate reason, why on earth had he not told her or at least introduced himself? He was certainly no one she had ever met before, for her circle of male acquaintances was very limited and if she had ever met him she would have remembered those piercing eyes, if not his coldly handsome face, for certain.

Then who on earth was he, and why did he want her presence at this Willerby place so desperately that he was even prepared to kidnap her forcibly? Linnet was pretty certain now that his motive was not seduction. And come to think of it, she thought, he did not look the kind of man who would give himself over to pure animal greed. His face had a kind of aloof, aesthetic air, cold even, more like a monk dedicated to self-denial than a pleasure-seeking fun-lover.

She felt calmer now. She did not believe he meant her any harm, but Otto, still watching her warily, was not of the same metal. He looked a coarse, hefty creature, not averse to violence if necessary. His heavy, peasant features and glowering scowl indicated that this was not a man with whom she could trifle.

The carriage thundered on through the night, and despite the soft cushions and obviously good springs Linnet began to feel an aching in her bones. This Willerby was a mighty long way out of London. She resolved to speak to Otto. If she showed herself pleasant and not angered by his roughness, perhaps he would relax and tell her something that might help to clear the mystery.

"Are we to go far?" she asked meekly. Otto just glowered. "I said have we much further to travel?" Linnet repeated. Otto shook his head and pursed his lips. She sighed. He was obviously under orders to say nothing. She tried once again. "Do you mind if I open the blinds? It is very stuffy in here." And indeed it was. She half-rose from the seat. Otto's hairy hand shot out and stopped her and he motioned her to sit again. Then he raised one blind with a grunt and sat down. Linnet gave up. He was not going to speak.

Through the aperture of the window she could see the silhouettes of trees and occasionally a cottage slip by. Heavens! They were deep in the countryside, miles away from London. How long had she been unconscious, she wondered. She remembered then the sickly-sweet smell. If she had been drugged she had possibly slept for hours. In that event, there was no means of guessing where they were or how far they had come.

The pace of the carriage had by now slackened considerably. Evidently the horses were tiring, so that would indicate they had travelled far. But in which direction? Willerby, Willerby. . . . No, it was no use.

She could not recollect having ever heard of such a place.

Otto's eyes were beginning to droop. It was the rhythmic rocking of his head from side to side with the motion of the carriage, thought Linnet, for she too was beginning to feel very drowsy. But, of course, it must be far into the night by now. She looked through the uncurtained window. Surely that faint grey streak ahead of them was early dawn light. If it were, then it would appear they were travelling eastwards.

The horses began to pick up speed again, as if they scented that their destination was near. Otto too shook his head and sat forward to look out of the window. Wherever Willerby might be, Linnet felt they must be approaching it. But from the window nothing yet was visible save a mist and an occasional very slight glimmer of light which no sooner appeared than it vanished again.

Suddenly the carriage stopped. Linnet heard the coachman jump down, then a hard metallic clang. A moment later the carriage rolled forward again, and Linnet caught sight of a huge iron gate set in a high wall, then the pathway was enclosed by trees. A drive up to a house, she guessed. Yes, the carriage wheels were crunching over gravel, and very soon the coach slewed round in a semi-circle and stopped.

Otto stood up and opened the door, then stepped down and turned to offer a hand to Linnet. She took it reluctantly, for the creature's hairy hand gave her a feeling of repulsion, and stepped carefully down.

And then the strange thing happened. As she looked

36

up at the great dark mass of the building before her, shrouded in thick ivy with huge eyes of windows and a gaping maw where the flight of shallow steps led up to the door, she had the strange, uncanny sensation that she recognised the place. But yet she knew she had never been here before. She gazed upwards. Against the lightening eastern sky a battlemented tower rose from each corner of the roof line of the house and the feeling of memory stirred again. Linnet felt almost as though she had once been here, and was now coming back to it.

Otto grunted impatiently as he waited at the foot of the steps. Linnet shook herself. Don't be ridiculous, she told herself firmly. You *know* you've never seen this place before. It's just the eerie appearance of the mansion in the glimmering light which is setting your over-vivid imagination to work, silly child. She went to join Otto.

The door at the head of the flight of steps opened as they reached it, and a woman with a shaded candle in her hand stood there. She looked as if she had just been aroused from sleep, for her eyes were heavy and she wore a woollen dressing-gown, and her grey hair was scraped up into curling-papers.

"I heard the carriage. I did not expect you back in the middle of the night, Otto," she commented. She was peering past him at Linnet, shading the glare of the candle from her eyes. But oddly enough, Linnet thought, it was not so much a curious stare as a hostile one. She did not seem unduly surprised to see a young woman brought into the house at this hour.

"Will you eat, Miss?" she asked Linnet. Despite the words, her tone implied complete unconcern.

Linnet shook her head. She had indeed been very hungry hours ago, but now fatigue had driven the need away.

"Then I'll take you up. I kept the bed warm and the room aired against your coming. You can get off to bed now too, Otto."

Otto lumbered away down a corridor from the vast entrance hall, and the woman led Linnet towards the stairs. Linnet followed her dully, her wits barely able to function, for she felt so sleepy.

The woman turned the knob of a panelled door and led Linnet into a bedroom. The polished parquet floor gleamed under the candlelight and Linnet made out a huge four-poster bed with rich hangings on the farther wall. Curiosity overcame her tiredness.

"Who are you?" she asked the woman, who was turning back the bedcovers. The woman raised her eyebrows.

"You don't remember me? Mrs Price, the house-keeper. You can't have forgotten me. It's only two years come Christmas. You can't have forgotten that soon."

Linnet stared at her. "Remember you?"

The old woman laughed, a dry, brittle laugh. "There's no doubting you'd like to have forgotten me, Miss Grey, and Willerby Manor too, no doubt at all. But here I am, and now here you are too."

She chuckled mirthlessly as she placed the candle on the table and padded back to the door. Linnet was utterly confused. How could she possibly remember a woman she was certain she had never seen before? And yet the woman had called her by her name. Could she possibly have forgotten? Mrs Price was still standing at the door.

"You called me by my name. How did you know it, for Otto did not tell you?"

"Otto tell me! That's a laugh!" cackled the woman. "How should I not know your name, that's what I'd like to know! Anyway, get to bed now, Miss Grey." She turned to go.

"But wait—tell me . . ." Linnet began.

"No questions," the woman muttered firmly. "The master gave strict orders."

"The master?"

The woman paused and looked back. "Go on, tell me you've forgotten him too," she sneered.

"I have indeed—if I ever knew him." Linnet sat on the edge of the high bed, wondering whether all this bizarre scene was really taking place or whether she was dreaming it all. Mrs Price sighed patiently.

"You knew him—and well too. But in case your adventures have driven him from your mind, let me refresh your memory."

"Yes—please do," Linnet cried.

"Why, he's Mr Bellamy, Miss Grey. You surely must remember Mr Marcus Bellamy."

"I fear I am somewhat confused, Mrs Price, and I don't understand at all," Linnet confessed.

"Then have a good sleep and maybe in the morning your mind will be fresh and clear," the woman said, and she closed the door. But before her footsteps padded away down the corridor Linnet heard the sound of a key being turned in the lock.

She rushed to the door and tried it, but it was securely locked. She recrossed the floor to the bed and felt her knees waver beneath her with fatigue. It was no use trying to escape in her present condition. It would be better to sleep in that vast, inviting bed, and in the morning when her brain had cleared she could think better how to act.

Linnet undressed and put on the voluminous flannelette nightgown that lay ready spread out on the bed, then blew out the candle. The bed was as comfortable as it looked, and within moments of climbing into it Linnet fell soundly asleep from sheer exhaustion.

FOUR

Linnet's sleep was haunted by strange dreams of opera-cloaked figures, shadowy and menacing, lurking in the darkness to fall upon her as she passed in endless dimly-lit streets; and huge, hairy-handed monsters pinioning her tightly. In her dreams she cried out for help, but no sound would issue from her lips. It was a terrifying nightmare, repeating itself endlessly over and over.

Linnet awoke and found herself bathed in perspiration and trembling from head to foot. A half-remembered scream lingered in her ears. Was it her own cry, dreamt but unreal, or had she cried out in her sleep? Or had she heard the eerie sound coming from another part of the vast, silent house?

She strained her ears to listen, but no sound could be heard save the creaking of floorboards and old furniture settling itself down. A far-away owl hooted dismally as it sought its nocturnal prey. Linnet felt still shaken and clambered down from the high bed and crossed to the window.

The heavy velvet drapes moved back noiselessly as she drew them apart, and from the high window she could see the dim outline of shrubs and trees. A hazy moon flitted behind banks of clouds, but even when it emerged, the scene was barely any clearer for a heavy mist lay close to the ground. Linnet shivered and hastened back to the warmth of the big old four-poster.

She lay curled in a ball, unable to go back to sleep immediately, for her feeling of unease still lingered. Mrs Price's odd words kept flashing through her mind. Was the woman somewhat crazed, or did she really believe she and Linnet had met before? She certainly spoke with calm certainty. Linnet wracked her memory, but in vain. She could swear Mrs Price was a total stranger to her. And the master she had mentioned too, this Mr Marcus Bellamy. No, the name Bellamy stirred no flicker of memory.

As Linnet lay tossing and turning over the woman's words in her mind, she caught sight of the grey square that was the bedroom window. No streak of dawn yet marked the sky, nor moonlight either. Then Linnet suddenly froze. A flicker of light, dim but unmistakable, crossed the window.

Linnet started upright, stifling the cry in her throat. The light did not reappear. But she was certain she had seen it, yet how was it possible so high above the garden below? For seconds Linnet sat frozen, terrified, then reason began to reassert itself. It was impossible. The bedroom was on the first floor and no one could have passed a light across her window. It must be her imagination, overwrought by the excitement of her abduction and added to fatigue, which had given rise to the vision. She really must take a grip on herself if she was to face the strange Mrs Price and remonstrate with her as-yet-unknown abductor on the morrow.

Yes, Mr Bellamy, Linnet thought, as she composed herself to sleep again; I shall have a few sharp words to speak to you for your unwarrantable behaviour. Her lips closed firmly as she turned her face into the pillow and fell asleep once again.

She awoke hours later and rubbed her eyes dreamily as consciousness returned. The unaccustomed feel of the soft mattress was the first sign that all was not as it should be, and, as Linnet sat up and stared in surprise at the rich folds of drapery around her bed, it all came back. She was no longer in her narrow little bed in the dormitory, but in a vast fourposter in some country mansion. As she remembered her visit to the theatre and the unexpected kidnapping by that huge brute Otto, the whole episode seemed like a nightmare brought on by a surfeit of heavy supper. But it was no dream. She was here, in a strange bed, in a strange room, in a strange house. And she had yet to meet her kidnapper, Otto's master.

Linnet rose quickly and ran across to the door, heedless of bare feet on a cold floor. The knob still would not yield. She was still imprisoned. She washed her face in the cold water in the ewer on the marble washstand and brushed her hair with one of the silver-backed brushes lying on the dressingtable. The cold water had refreshed her. Linnet's mind raced furiously as she brushed.

Why was she here? What motive had this Marcus Bellamy for grabbing her forcibly and bringing her here? If he was labouring under the mistaken idea that her family or a wealthy relative would grant him a large sum by way of ransom, then he was vastly mistaken. She had not a living relative remaining, so far as she knew, and none to notice her disappearance save possibly Madame Roland. And even Madame would probably only click her tongue with annoyance at Linnet's non-reappearance last night and immediately engage the new teacher to replace her. She would doubtless take it that since she had virtually given notice to Linnet, her ungrateful pupil-teacher had maliciously deserted her to find another post. It was unlikely she would even report Linnet's disappearance to the police.

Even if she did, it was unlikely they would even be able to trace her, for no one had known she was going to the theatre, so no enquiries would be instituted there. Any search would be bound to lead to a dead end.

So she could expect no help from Madame's quarter. To escape, then, would be up to herself. But where was she? It was difficult to know how to return to London, alone and without even sufficient money in her purse for a rail fare, when she did not even know in which county she was.

Linnet put down the hairbrush and crossed to the window. The sky was still grey and drear—a typical winter sky. A solitary gull wheeled and dipped and uttered a shrill squawk now and again.

A seagull! Linnet realised with a start that if it was indeed a seagull, then she could not be very far inland from the coast, and the length of the carriage journey from London would indicate that this must be Kent or Essex. It could hardly be further from London, unless she had been unconscious for longer on the journey than she knew. But could she be sure that the bird, which had now wheeled away and out of sight, was indeed a gull? Most of her life had been spent in London's fog and grime, far from the country and the lore of countryfolk. True, London held many birds, pigeons and starlings on every rooftop, and she remembered seeing this shrieking, swooping bird occasionally on her rare walks by the Embankment when Madame had allowed her an afternoon off. But was it a seabird?

She searched her memory. Somewhere something prickled, eager to come alive. She felt sure she had not recognised the bird by chance. And then she remembered. It was one of those far-off beloved days of childhood when her father, handsome and bronzed and sparkling-eyed, had come home from one of his lengthy trips. He had danced his little girl on his knee and told her captivating tales of far-away exotic countries and strange birds and beasts and oddly-costumed people.

But amidst the excitement of foreign lands, he had talked also of long journeys, of storms that terrified even the hardiest sailor, and one of which he little knew was to claim his and his pretty wife's lives one day, and of the days not long gone of the sailing ships, when sailors dreaded being becalmed, when not a breeze stirred the surface of the still oceans. Linnet the child had listened open-mouthed to his eager, vivid tales, though his wife sat by and gazed into space,

47

hardly listening, as though she too was far away in a distant land. Not a word that fell from her father's lips had Linnet missed, and now she remembered his words about the seagulls; how they alighted to rest on the mast of his beloved ship, the *Linnet*, grateful for a respite on their long journey across the endless seas.

He had described the birds in detail, their ravening mouths and manners, and their coarse, demanding shrieks. He had mimicked the sounds they made, and even now Linnet could hear the sound in her ears. That was why she had known the bird outside in the grey November sky was a seagull.

She brushed the golden memory of her father from her mind. It hurt to remember how loved and cherished she had felt then. That was before the beautiful mother with the faraway look always in her eyes had gone away with him, never to return. That was the hurtful memory—that her mother had relinquished her in favour of the dashing sea captain, the husband she adored.

Linnet shivered. It was cold in the bedroom. She took off the thick nightgown and put on her warm merino dress. Even then she was still cold, so she wrapped her ulster about her and sat on the edge of the bed. Someone must come soon to release her.

Before many minutes elapsed, she heard soft footsteps approaching the door. A key turned in the lock. Linnet hastened towards the door. Mrs Price came in carrying a tray which she deposited on the washstand, turning to lock the door immediately.

"Here you are, Miss, a bowl of nice hot porridge to warm you up, and tea and bread and butter," she announced as she pushed the key safely into the depths of her apron pocket. She eyed Linnet with a firm, obstinate look that seemed to say, 'And we'll have no nonsense from you, either.' Linnet, who had been about to demand authoritatively that she be given an explanation for being here, decided that perhaps that would not be the best way to gain any information from Mrs Price after all. A softer line of approach was called for.

"Thank you," she said gently. "I am indeed cold, and hot porridge would be most welcome." She took the bowl and sat on the edge of the bed, cradling its warmth in her hands. Before she began to spoon it, however, she looked up at the housekeeper appealingly. "But I fear I am most confused, Mrs Price. You seem to know who I am, but I do not understand at all why I am here."

She hoped the questioning note in her voice would entice the woman to explain, but it seemed to have the opposite effect. Mrs Price pursed her thin lips tightly and threw back her sparse, wispy hair unnecessarily, her jaw tightening and indicating that Linnet would gain little from her.

"Please," said Linnet coaxingly. "Perhaps I have forgotten something I ought to have remembered, but I fear this whole situation makes no sense to me at all. I beg you to tell me what you know."

Mrs Price appeared to hesitate fractionally, then she stiffened again. "I have my orders, Miss Grey, and I'm not one to disobey. No doubt Mr Bellamy will say all that needs to be said when he comes. It's for him to speak to you, not me."

She turned to the door purposefully and unlocked it. As she was about to close it behind her, she turned again. "Seeing as it's so cold, I'll have a fire lit up here for you, Miss. I'll send Cissie up to see to it."

Before Linnet could reply, the key had turned in the lock and Mrs Price's footsteps were retreating down the corridor. Linnet ate her porridge thoughtfully. Then, warmed and refreshed by the hot tea also, she felt considerably more comfortable.

The door opened again, and a young, plump maid-servant hurried in carrying a scuttle of coals with paper and firewood on top. She put the scuttle down hastily and relocked the door before advancing cautiously towards the fireplace, keeping her wide blue eyes warily fixed on Linnet. Linnet smiled at her and the girl dropped her gaze, fumbling clumsily with the newspaper as she screwed it up into firelighters.

"Hullo," said Linnet amiably, hoping to gain more from the maid than she had from the housekeeper. "You're Cissie, aren't you?"

The girl nodded without looking up at her and carried on screwing the paper and arranging it in the empty grate. Linnet sighed. It would appear she had been ordered not to speak to the house-guest. Linnet decided to try other tactics.

"Come here, Cissie," she said in the stern but not unkindly voice she used in the classroom, a voice that implied that instant obedience was expected. Cissie reacted like any maid. She rose from her knees, rubbed her dusty hands clean on her apron, and came to stand submissively before Linnet, who still sat on the edge of the bed.

"Yes, Miss?"

"How old are you, Cissie?"

"Sixteen, Miss."

"Do you like working here?"

Cissie shrugged her shoulders and groped for words. "Ain't got much choice, Miss. There's little work for girls in the village, and me being the eldest of seven, my dad says I'll work here, so I do."

"What village, Cissie?"

The maid raised her pale eyes and looked at Linnet in surprise. Linnet could see she was wondering how a guest could be so ignorant.

"Why, Willerby, of course, Miss. Being so far away from town and all, it's not easy to get work. And if I don't get the fire lit and get back down to the kitchen to help do the vegetables, I'll not have this position for long. Can I go now, Miss?"

The pale eyes were beseeching. Linnet felt sorry for the girl. "Yes, of course. I shall be glad of a fire."

As Cissie laid the sticks of wood carefully criss-cross over the paper and then balanced the pieces of coal on top, Linnet watched her thoughtfully. Willerby was a village, then, but where?

"Cissie," she said in as casual a manner as she could. "What county is Willerby in?"

Cissie looked up sharply from the fire, which was now starting to crackle and burn merrily. "What county is Willerby in?" she repeated, a look of complete perplexity on her pleasant, round face. "What funny questions you do ask, Miss! Why, Essex, of course!" A frown crossed her forehead. "But Mrs Price told me plain I wasn't to talk to you, Miss, not

51

answer no questions nor tell you anything. So please don't talk to me again or you'll get me in awful trouble."

She swept up the hearth, then hastened to go, to be out of temptation's way. Linnet sensed that the girl was not unfriendly and cold as Mrs Price had been, but only fearful for her job. Perhaps, with a little more incentive, she could reveal more. She might even have overheard something or know why Linnet had been brought here.

Linnet remembered she still had a couple of sixpences in her reticule. She took one out and called to the girl as she was about to unlock the door.

"Cissie, wait a moment." She crossed to her, and the maid stood wavering, uncertain what to do.

Linnet pressed the coin into her hand. "Cissie, I need help," she said softly. "I need help more than I have ever done. Will you be a friend to me?"

Cissie cast a terrified glance behind her at the locked door. "I can't, Miss. I dursn't! Mrs Price'll beat me if I let you go! Oh, no, Miss, please. Let me go! I don't want your money!" She began to wail, blubbering noisily into the hem of her apron.

Linnet patted her arm. "There, there, it's all right, Cissie. I'm not asking you to let me escape. But you do know I'm a prisoner here, don't you?"

The girl nodded dumbly.

"Do you know why?"

Cissie shook her head vigorously, blowing her nose and wiping her eyes on her apron.

"Are you sure, Cissie? Have you not heard Mr Bellamy say anything about it?"

"No, Miss. I haven't met the master yet. I only started work here a month ago and Mr. Bellamy doesn't often come down here."

"Where is he, then?"

"At his business in London."

"I see. So you don't know what he looks like, or what manner of man he is?"

"No, not really. I know he's a lawyer, a very important man, so Mrs Price told me, but I won't see him till he comes home today. Oh, Miss, I got to hurry. There's so much to do before the master gets back."

"Very well, Cissie, but one word more. Have you heard Mrs Price say why I am here?"

"She ain't told me nothing. But I did hear her talking to that big Otto. He never says anything, but she talks to him a lot down in the kitchen. I keep out of the way when Otto's there 'cause he frightens me."

Linnet knew what the girl meant. Otto's big, lumbering frame and his surly silence would frighten anyone. "What did you hear Mrs Price say to him, Cissie?" she prompted.

Cissie dropped her apron and turned her big, tearful eyes on Linnet. "She told him she was glad Mr Bellamy was bringing Miss Grey home after all this time, she said, 'cause you was a very wicked person, and she for one would be very glad to see you punished."

Cissie grabbed up the coal-scuttle and hurried out, before Linnet could recover her breath.

FIVE

Linnet scarcely heard the key turn in the lock or Cissie's frightened footsteps scuttling away down the corridor. She was too shocked and bemused at the maid's words. What did she mean about Bellamy bringing her home here, as if this gloomy house had ever been her home. She had never ever visited the place before.

And to be punished, Mrs Price had said. Punished? For what? What had she ever done to offend this Marcus Bellamy, or anyone else for that matter? Was it possible she could have met him and slighted him in some way, perhaps quite unintentionally? It seemed unlikely, for Linnet's movements had been very restricted, living only in Madame's Academy, and very rarely leaving it.

And even if she had somehow occasioned him some annoyance, what manner of man was this Marcus Bellamy, that he could bear so strong a grudge that he would go to such extreme lengths to pay her out? He could be no normal man. Linnet shuddered at the thought that maybe she was to deal with a lunatic.

Cissie had said that he was to come today, so very soon Linnet would have the opportunity to demand of him what he intended, and the reason why he had kidnapped her so rudely. She recalled the handsome, tight-lipped face of the man outside the theatre. He had certainly looked determined and cold, ruthless even, but was he truly a madman? Neither his face nor his name, Bellamy, stirred even a vestige of a memory in Linnet's mind. She was certain she had never at any time had any dealings with this man. So what was all this talk of bringing her home, and of punishing her for her misdeeds? Perhaps Cissie, who was decidedly on the dull side, had got it all wrong. All that Linnet could do in the circumstances was to wait and see.

Wait. She tried the door half-heartedly, but it was still firmly locked, so she had no alternative but to wait. Linnet crossed to the window again and looked out at the wintry sky, still grey and chill and empty. She drew back the heavy lace curtain that obscured the lower half of the window, the better to see the garden below.

Linnet caught her breath. From the window she could see little of the garden below, only a far high wall and misty open country beyond. But her surprise was on seeing that her vision was limited by a narrow balcony outside her window, little more than a parapet. It was bounded on the outer side by a low stone wall where lichens gleamed green in the crevices.

Linnet craned her head. The balcony appeared to stretch both to right and left of her window. If it ran right along the house wall, then it was possible that someone had walked along it last night and the flickering light which had crossed the window was real and no figment of her overtired imagination.

But why should someone pass the window, high above the ground, on a narrow ledge? Not to check on her, surely, for the light had passed quickly without pausing.

The doorknob rattled behind her. Linnet turned as Mrs Price swept in. This time she did not relock the door behind her, but stood just inside the room and watched Linnet guardedly. Linnet decided to beat about the bush no longer.

"That balcony outside; who walks along there at night with a light?" she demanded, and saw the housekeeper blanch suddenly.

"A light? I—I don't know, Miss Grey," Mrs Price stuttered, then Linnet saw her face change, tightening as she drew herself up. "I came to tell you news, not to answer questions," she said in a staccato voice. "Mr Bellamy will be home this evening and I will permit you to leave this room and return to your own, so that you may prepare. But you must give me your word that there'll be no monkey business."

She glared at Linnet defiantly. "Monkey business?" repeated Linnet. "What do you mean?"

"I know your mischievous ways, Miss Grey, and I want none of your tricks. Promise me—though whether your promises mean anything I doubt—but promise me you won't try to run away."

Linnet stared at her. "What on earth do you mean?"

The woman's lip curled in a sneer. "You know full

well what I mean, Miss, and don't go trying to act the innocent with me, with me of all people!"

Linnet spread her hands. "I'm afraid I'm quite at a loss to understand you at all. Your talk of my wickedness makes no sense to me at all."

"Then swear you won't run away—again."

Again? Linnet was becoming more and more confused. What was the woman blathering about? Mrs Price was standing, hands on hips, awaiting an answer.

"Remember the marshes out there," the housekeeper went on warningly. "I know you found your way through somehow two years ago, but it won't be safe to risk it again. Them marshes have claimed many a man's life, and you was very lucky to get away through them. Now tell me for certain that you'll stay within the house, and I'll let you out of this room."

Linnet could barely follow a word of what the woman was saying, but she grasped that to agree would grant her comparative freedom. This room was dull and cheerless despite the glowing fire.

"I'll gladly promise what you ask, Mrs Price," she told her, "for there are matters I wish to discuss with Mr Bellamy when he comes. I certainly want to stay at least until I have seen him."

She saw the housekeeper's visible relief. "Very well," Mrs Price said in considerably gentler tones, and opened the door for Linnet to pass. Linnet picked up her reticule and went out.

A long, oak-panelled corridor stretched in both directions, ending at a small window to the left, and reaching the balustraded head of a wide staircase to the right. Linnet hesitated, waiting for Mrs Price to show her where she was to go. Mrs Price stood watching her, swinging a bunch of keys in her hand.

"You may go to your own room, as I said, Miss Grey. And after you are dressed and ready, you may go down to the library if you wish. Just so long as you don't go outside, you may go where you will."

The housekeeper moved to the head of the stairs and then turned, her hand on the carved balustrade. "Just one thing," she added as an afterthought. "Because I know you and your deceitfulness, I have asked Otto to keep an eye on you, so to attempt to cheat me would be useless."

With a quick swish of skirts, she was gone. Linnet stood irresolute, wondering what to do. She had spoken the truth when she had told Mrs Price that she wanted to wait and see Marcus Bellamy, so that she could find out what this mad conspiracy was all about, so there was little point in attempting to escape —yet. But she knew not where to go. To her own room, Mrs Price had said, but where was this room, supposedly hers, to be found? There was only one way to find out.

Linnet walked along the gloomy, ill-lit corridor, and tried the handle of the first door she came to. It was only a large storage room, a kind of boxroom with no window and filled with an assortment of brooms and dustpans. The second door was locked. The third yielded to her hand.

Linnet opened it and went in. It was a handsomely-furnished bedroom with sombre drapes and very simply decorated, evidently a man's room, for a pair of men's tortoise-shell-backed brushes lay on the dressing-table and a folded razor and shaving-brush. The high bed was unmade. It was obviously not the room she sought. Marcus Bellamy's room, perhaps?

Out of curiosity, Linnet crept right into the room quietly, leaving the door ajar so that she would hear the sound of anyone coming. She examined the room quickly, anxious to try and discover something of the eccentric man who had kidnapped her, but the room was devoid of any telltale evidence. No photographs decorated the furniture or walls. No papers lay in the drawers, only neatly-folded clothes. The wardrobe contained an assortment of suits and frock-coats and a rack of tasteful stocks and cravats, and emanated a masculine, virile odour. No, there was nothing here to betray the character of the man Bellamy.

Then she spotted the small secretaire in the corner by the window. Ah! Here, if anywhere, would be his most personal belongings—papers, letters, diaries, even. But to her disappointment the secretaire was securely locked. He was evidently a careful man, this Marcus Bellamy. Cissie had said he was a lawyer, and it was no doubt in his training to be careful and methodical in everything.

Linnet closed the door after her and went on along the corridor. If he was so methodical it hardly fitted in with the impression she had had up to now of a crazed lunatic. It didn't make sense.

Cissie came bustling along from the staircase end of the corridor, her arms laden with piles of bedlinen. She looked askance at Linnet, standing idly in the corridor. Linnet decided she had better bluff.

"O, Cissie, I wonder whether you heard Mrs Price say whether Miss Grey's room was still the same, or whether it had been changed?"

"Oh, no, Miss, it's still the one at the end." Cissie nodded towards the end door on the left by way of indication, and hurried into the room Linnet had just left. Linnet went on and entered the room Cissie had indicated.

But who was she, this mysterious Miss Grey they aloud with pleasure at the sight that met her eyes. It was a beautiful room, with a high bed draped in a white velvet coverlet, and with white velvet curtains at the window tied back with blue ribbons. The carved dressing-table was surrounded by luxurious peach-coloured brocade, and the stool before it was upholstered with the same material. Silver brushes and cutglass dishes and trays covered the top of the dressing-table and a deep fur rug lay on the thick Turkish carpet alongside the bed. A fire crackled in the wide hearth, and its light was caught and reflected by well-burnished copper lamps on the walls. It was a pretty, feminine room, in strong contrast to the stark, masculine one she had just left.

Whoever had owned this room and ordered its decoration was certainly a person with an eye for taste and comfort, Linnet thought, and someone to whom expense was no object. It was just such a room as she would have chosen for herself, if only she had been rich. It must be a woman who loved pretty things and adorning herself before the pier-glass mirror who had once lived there.

But for her unusual situation she could have cried

spoke of? Linnet ran a critical eye over a glass-fronted cabinet by the window. It contained a huge assortment of dolls, minute and beautifully-costumed, and pebbles and sea-shells of every hue. It seemed more like the collection of a child than a woman. Was the owner only a very young girl, then? Had she grown to womanhood and still retained the mind of a child?

A huge chest of drawers next to the cabinet caught Linnet's eye. Curiosity overcame her feelings of propriety and although she felt slightly guilty at opening drawers belonging to someone else, she persuaded herself that it was in her own protection. She had learnt little about her captor from the other room, so maybe here she would learn something. . . .

But the drawers contained only women's clothes, pretty underskirts and chemises of far finer materials than Linnet had ever known. And stockings and gloves and fans, all the paraphernalia of a pampered young woman, but no clue as to her identity.

Linnet turned with a guilty start as the door opened, but it was Cissie who came in and bobbed a curtsey with no sign of having noticed anything amiss.

"Have you got all you want, Miss? Do you want hot water or anything? I think you'll find all your frocks in the wardrobe are pressed and ready, if you want to change. Will there be anything else?"

"Thank you, no, Cissie. I think I shall manage quite well." Linnet managed to keep her voice calm, as if she had not been caught prying.

"Lunch will be in half an hour, Mrs Price says I'm to tell you."

"Thank you, Cissie." As the girl turned to go, Linnet hurried towards her. "But let me ask you first, Cissie . . ."

"No, Miss, I'm sorry. Mrs Price was cross with me for lingering so long before. She said definitely this time I was to answer no questions, or I'd pay for it."

Cissie turned and went out resolutely. Linnet sighed and went back to the wardrobe. She felt very bedraggled now in her one and only dress. Maybe she would take advantage of the offer of a freshly-pressed one, especially if she was to meet this Bellamy man later today.

She opened the wardrobe door to take stock of the frocks available. She could not help the gasp, melting into a sigh of ecstatic envy that escaped her, for the wardrobe was crammed with cloaks and furs and dresses of every kind. Many of the dresses were fragile as gossamer, the kind of gown that one could wear only to a very formal and special occasion. And even the day-gowns were elaborately and expensively trimmed and ruched, and made of the very finest mohair and moire and taffeta. Every one boasted bugle beads or fine lace of crochet work. There was not a plain, simple one amongst them.

Linnet breathed a deep sigh of envy. How few girls could afford such a wardrobe of magnificent clothes. The girl who owned this room was a lucky creature indeed.

She selected a frock of dove-grey, the demurest she could find, and laid it on the bed, then quickly unbuttoned her own frock and slipped it off. The dove-grey fitted perfectly. It was quite amazing, almost as if it had been specially tailored for her. Linnet turned and twisted before the long pier-glass, admiring and approving her reflection.

Then she glanced back with a longing, wistful look at the wardrobe. It would be fun to try on one of the truly beautiful, regal gowns meant for evening wear. And there was still half an hour to lunch, so it was unlikely she would be disturbed.

Linnet yielded to the temptation. Never again, probably, would she have occasion to wear a creation of such magnificence. She lifted down a frothy pale-blue confection, so airy and light she almost feared her fingers would penetrate its fineness. She held it up before her body and savoured the feel of its dewy elegance against her skin. The picture in the pier-glass was breathtaking. She had never believed she could look so lovely, for the ethereal paleness of the gown enhanced her auburn hair to a fiery magnificence. On a whim, Linnet pulled out the hairpins and let her hair fall in thick curls about her shoulders. She pirouetted with sheer pleasure before the mirror. If only Madame and the girls could see her now!

But then the chuckle of pleasure died in her throat. Through the mirror she caught sight of a face, and she spun round guiltily. But it was not Cissie or Mrs Price leaning leisurely on the door, but a man. It was the man outside the theatre—Marcus Bellamy. Linnet coloured furiously and tried to hide behind the frothy blue dress.

He smiled slowly, but there was no warmth in the smile, for his eyes were cold and their power seemed to bore into her. He folded his arms, making no attempt to apologise and withdraw.

"I see you have not changed, my dear, he said in a cool, drawling voice. "You are every bit as vain and shallow as you were. I could have hoped that time would have improved you, but I see I was wrong to hope it. You are still the selfish, empty-headed creature that you always were."

SIX

Linnet was stupefied, both by Bellamy's sudden, totally unexpected appearance and by his strange, cold, completely nonsensical words. But before she could gather her wits and regain her composure, half-dressed as she was, he had pulled himself upright lazily from the doorjamb and closed the door behind him, leaving her to try to sort out what his enigmatical words had implied.

What did he mean, saying she was just as vain and selfish as she used to be? He spoke as if he had known her before, and known her well, too. And so had Mrs Price. Were they all crazy in this house, acting as if they knew and despised her, when she knew for certain she had never met any of them before—except Bellamy the previous night at the theatre?

It was all too ridiculous for words. Linnet dressed slowly in the dove-grey frock, and resolved that she would not linger in this house in order to discover the reason for her being brought here. She would tell Bellamy forcibly at lunch that there must have been some hideous mistake, and if he would be pleased to let her go, she would return to London at once.

But how? She had only a sixpence left in her purse,

nowhere near enough for a train fare. Perhaps if she could convince Bellamy of his mistake he would be chivalrous enough to pay her fare, or send her back in the carriage. But suppose he refused? Suppose he knew well enough who she was and had some devious plan in his scheming mind?

Linnet brushed the thought aside. She would face that obstacle if and when she came to it. But one thing was certain—she wanted to get away from this gloomy old house and its crazy occupants as soon as she possibly could.

From somewhere below, a gong sounded as Linnet was putting the finishing touches to dressing her hair. She left the room and went along the corridor, down the wide staircase and turned along a smaller corridor till she reached an oak-panelled door. It was only as she put her hand on the knob that she realised she had known, almost instinctively, the way to the dining-room. She opened the door to confirm her thoughts. A long table laid with a white damask cloth and lit with a central candelabra met her gaze. Now how had she known how to find the room, out of all the doors she had passed in order to reach it? Suddenly then she remembered the inexplicable feeling of familiarity she had felt when she first stood on the steps outside the manor last night. It was an uneasy sensation that sent a momentary shiver shuddering through her. Linnet rejected it firmly and went in.

There was no one else yet at table. Linnet sat down uneasily. It was an odd experience. She had definitely known, as if by a sixth sense, the way to come. Was it after all *she* who was perhaps a little crazed? Had she really been in this house before and now had no recollection of the event?

She was still blinking unbelievingly in the candlelight, refusing to admit the possibility that she could be so confused, when Cissie came in with a tureen of soup. Having set it down on the table, she then poured one bowl for Linnet and made to leave.

Linnet looked at her enquiringly. "Is no one else coming to lunch, Cissie?"

The girl shook her head, her mouth firmly closed.

"What of Mr. Bellamy, then?"

Cissie glanced about her before answering. "He's taking lunch in his room. And I'm not to talk to you, Miss Grey."

She had gone before Linnet could open her mouth again. The room beyond the candle's reach was gloomy, despite the fact that it was still only midday. Heavy rain pounded ceaselessly against the windows. Linnet ate in silence. Cissie came to clear away the soup plate and serve the meat course, but her tightly-compressed lips showed her determination not to speak and deterred Linnet from questioning her further.

Why, wondered Linnet, was Bellamy lunching alone? Was he tired from the journey, or did he hate her, or the girl he thought she was, so much that he preferred to avoid her company? Whatever the reason, Linnet felt very lonely and just a little afraid. Bellamy was so cold and sneering and he had such a hard set to his otherwise handsome face, that he appeared to be capable of dealing out severity, if not cruelty. She had yet to discover how he intended to treat her—and why.

Cissie cleared away the dishes, still in stubborn silence, and Linnet was left alone. She decided she might as well investigate the rest of the house rather than sit here alone and apparently forgotten. Out in the corridor the same sensation came over her as before—the door to the left was the library, she knew. She looked inside. It was a large, high-ceilinged room lined with bookshelves, and all the shelves were crammed with expensively-bound books. A large solid desk dominated the centre of the deep Turkish carpet. Linnet shivered as she closed the door again and turned towards the entrance vestibule.

It was strange, uncanny in the extreme, but she definitely knew where each corridor led from here. That one to the right would lead to a glass-roofed conservatory alongside the east wall of the house, she could swear it. And there at the end of the corridor, a glass door led into exactly the conservatory she had visualised, crowded with plants and shrubs and smelling heavily of tropical blooms.

Linnet retraced her footsteps to the vestibule. By now she was trembling. Were these people right? Had she truly been here before, and some accident had robbed her of her memory? What else could account for her knowing the lay-out of the house, almost as if she had once lived here?

It was a frightening thought, that these odd people, Bellamy and Mrs Price, might know more of her past than she did herself. And there was an atmosphere of repressed menace in this house that caused Linnet to shudder yet more. She must get away from here, and quickly, before some harm would befall her!

A sudden click behind her made Linnet start and turn hurriedly, just in time to see the green baize door leading to the servants' quarters closing quietly. Linnet had the distinct impression that someone had been standing close behind her, watching to see if she betrayed her earlier knowledge of this place, which she had hitherto denied.

No one came near Linnet all afternoon, but still the sensation that she was being watched accompanied her everywhere. She passed the time by going all over the house, upstairs and down, and found that only certain parts of the house had that strange feeling of familiarity. Most of the rooms upstairs gave no sensation at all beyond one of feeling rather regretful that such a noble old house should be so neglected. Unused rooms lay silent and dusty, festooned with cobwebs and smelling dank and unaired. Trunks and piles of papers lay rotting in a little boxroom. Most of the rooms were unlocked, save for one heavy oak door studded with iron nails set in an arched recess at the end of the corridor near her own room. Because it was so near the window in the outer wall, Linnet judged it could only be a very small room beyond the door and probably of little importance.

Each time she returned to the vestibule the old feeling of intense familiarity returned. Linnet passed through it as quickly as possible, for the experience made her feel decidedly uneasy and not a little afraid.

By the evening, Linnet was growing more

venturesome. Wherever she wandered, no one came to restrain her, although she sensed she was still being watched.

At last the thought came. If no one was close enough to stop her, or if they had ceased to worry about her, perhaps she could take the opportunity while they were occupied to slip out of the house. Perhaps if she could get as far as the village she could explain her predicament to someone who would help, lend her the fare home. . . .

Linnet looked out of the window. It was still raining, though not so heavily as before. She would have to go up and fetch her ulster. It was far too cold and wet to go out in only her dress.

On the way to her bedroom and back Linnet encountered no one. She carried her reticule rolled up in her ulster and hoped that if she met someone the bundle under her arm might go unnoticed.

The vestibule was empty. Linnet felt the odd shiver run up her spine again as she crossed it and mounted the two marble steps to the front door. She glanced back at the green baize door, which remained stolid and unmoving. It seemed they were no longer watching.

Linnet gripped the doorknob and turned it, hoping the door would not creak on its iron hinges. It swung open easily, but as Linnet made to dart out, a huge, shadowy figure lumbered towards her from out of the night and blocked her way, causing her to gasp with shock. The big figure towered tall and unmoving before her, and the night air was heavy with a sickly sweet smell. Linnet gave a strangled shriek and

76

slammed the door, ran back across the vestibule and up the stairs.

Back in the comparative safety of her bedroom, Linnet sank on the bed, gasping with fright and out of breath, but no footsteps followed her. The house remained as menacingly silent as before. Linnet grew more and more afraid.

What were they trying to do to her, leaving her alone so long, and refusing to answer her questions even when someone did come? Were they trying to drive her out of her mind? And why? What reason could they possibly have for treating a perfect stranger in this way?

But was she a stranger? Mrs Price and Bellamy behaved as if they knew her well. Cissie, admittedly, was new to the house, but even Otto, the silent, uncommunicative one, was undoubtedly on the side of Bellamy, for it was he who had obeyed the order to kidnap her, and who was obviously ordered to watch her every move now. Oh, what was all this about? Linnet lay on the bed, wracking her brain to find the answer, but none came.

Linnet was beginning to feel sleep creeping over her when suddenly she was jerked awake by the hollow sound of the gong booming again downstairs. She sat upright. Of course! It was time for dinner! No time now to change her dress again. She tidied her hair quickly at the mirror and hurried out into the corridor. Now, perhaps, she would have the opportunity at last to speak to this man Bellamy and demand her release.

As she turned from the vestibule into the corridor

towards the dining-room, she had a brief glimpse of a man's back as he disappeared into the library and closed the door. Linnet smiled grimly. So Bellamy was trying to elude her again. Well, this time he would not escape. She marched firmly to the library door, tapped, and entered without waiting for an invitation to enter.

Marcus Bellamy sat at the desk facing her, his dark, handsome face illuminated by the lamp before him. He arched his black brows in question as Linnet stood in the doorway.

"Well?" he demanded, and despite his curtness Linnet detected a gentleness in his tone. But in her determination to clear up this matter and be released from his clutches, she had no time to waste to ponder over unexpected glimpses of humanity in the man.

"It is I who should demand 'Well' of you, sir," she said crisply. "Would you be so kind as to render an immediate explanation of your behaviour, Mr Bellamy, and tell me what is the reason for your behaviour?"

A crooked smile flickered on Bellamy's lips. He leaned forward and put his elbows on the desk, arching his fingertips together in steeple fashion and regarding her curiously. He made no effort to answer. Linnet grew angry.

"Do you hear me, sir? I demand an explanation and an apology. That done, you may return me to London with all speed before a search is instituted, if it has not already been done."

Bellamy put his head on one side, still smiling

wryly. He looked like a slow-witted child trying hard to understand its teacher's words. Linnet fumed. He was playing some kind of game with her and she was furious.

"For heaven's sake, man, speak! Have you lost your tongue?"

Bellamy laid his hands flat on the table and the wry smile fled. "When you give me the opportunity, Miss, there is much I could say. But I do not propose to discuss any matter with you at present, but to give you time to quieten down and ponder. Later, then, we may talk. Until then, I have nothing to say to you, Miss Grey."

Linnet gasped. "Quieten down and ponder?" she repeated in amazement. "Ponder what, may I ask?"

The smile, humourless and grim, reappeared briefly. "You do not need me to tell you that, I am sure. Go now, and after dinner return to your room. I do not wish to see you until I send for you."

Linnet gasped again at the man's audacity. He— send for her! The temerity of the creature! She opened her mouth to demonstrate, But Bellamy was glaring at her, his lips now unsmiling and taut. "Go," he said curtly.

Years of submissiveness led Linnet to turn and pull the door close behind her, tears of frustration welling in her eyes. At the last moment she turned.

"Please, Mr Bellamy," she pleaded earnestly. "I truly have no conception of what you mean. I beg you to explain to me what is happening, for I am so confused."

Bellamy looked surprised for a moment, his hand stopping half-way as he went to put a taper to his pipe. Then a gleam of understanding seemed to flicker in those dark, uncompromising eyes.

"You have not changed, my dear," he commented with a sigh. "From the raging virago to the meek maid in the twinkling of an eye, but you do not dupe me now. Not any more."

He turned sharply to the bookshelves and busied himself selecting a volume. His straight, unyielding back showed he had done with her. Bemused, Linnet closed the door.

She ate dinner in a daze. His words made no more sense to her than his earlier ones. Alone in her room again, she lay on the bed and turned over and over in her mind what Bellamy had said, but nothing made sense at all. At last, exhausted with worry and still frightened, she fell into a fitful sleep.

Not many minutes seemed to have elapsed before Linnet suddenly awoke again, but she did not know what it was that had awakened her. She sat upright and realised she had been so tired that she had fallen asleep on top of the quilted coverlet without even undressing. She swung her legs over the side of the bed and began to undress. But even as her fingers unfastened the top button of her bodice, she suddenly stiffened with fear. Far away but unmistakable was the sound of a cry, a piercing wail that echoed faintly up and down the corridors of Willerby Manor.

SEVEN

Linnet's heart faltered for a second before it began to thud noisily again. Then there was silence, complete and unbroken. Not a sound stirred the night air. No footstep shredded the quiet, no one came running to investigate the source of the cry. Then suddenly it came again, quavering higher and shriller this time, and Linnet's heart thudded.

The sound wavered and died away. It was not the cry of an animal in pain, but a human cry. Nor was it outside in the night, but here, in Willerby Manor. And no one seemed to notice or to care. Were they all deaf or just uncaring? Whatever the reason, Linnet could not remain unmoved. The cry was infinitely haunting and pathetic. Somewhere in this vast, gloomy old house someone was in need, and Linnet could not resist the desire to go and seek that person, fearful though she was. Someone was in pain or in distress, and Linnet knew only too well from her own experience the bitterness of being left to suffer alone. Whoever the creature was, he or she was in need of comfort, Linnet felt sure, and she could not leave him to bear the pangs alone.

The night air was cold on her shoulders. She

groped for her dressing-gown in the dark and found it lying on the bed where she had draped it. Then she lit the candle in its silver holder on the night table beside the bed and by its dim light she opened the door. The corridor was deserted and silent and as dark as a tomb. Linnet carried the candle aloft and walked timidly out, uncertain which way to go in search. The sound had seemed to come from the left, but in that direction lay only the door by the window, and that had been locked. Linnet approached the heavy door, and was surprised to see in the flickering light that it now stood slightly ajar. Could the cry have come from this small room?

Her hand touched the cold iron knob and pushed the heavy door slowly open. The candle flame sputtered. A draught of air from within was threatening to extinguish it. Linnet shielded the tiny glow with her hand until it resumed strength, and peered into the darkness beyond. Soon her gaze made out the carved shape of an iron handrail, mounting steeply from just within the door and circling sharply above her head. It was a spiral staircase.

Of course! She realised now that this small room was in fact the landing for the staircase rising to one of the battlemented towers on each corner of the manor that she had noticed the night she arrived. And it was the draught down the narrow stairway which had threatened to put out the candle. Had those plaintive cries come from up there, high in a tower room?

Linnet debated whether to ascend or not. If the candle were to blow out she had no means to relight it unless she returned to her room, and in the dark she

84

would be unlikely to find the person in distress. As she hovered, uncertain, in the doorway, she became aware of something strange that was troubling her. Then she placed it. It was the sweet, cloying smell she had detected earlier, when she had tried to escape through the front door.

Linnet turned and the smell in the corridor grew stronger. Whatever it was was out here, for the breeze on the narrow staircase would have wafted away any odour coming from there. Linnet felt uneasy. She sensed that she was not alone in the corridor, though she could hear and see nothing. The sweet scent originated from someone standing there in the darkness, she felt certain, and it was surely not the scent of a woman's perfume.

Linnet shivered. It was frightening to stand in the small arc of light thrown from her candle, knowing she was visible to the silent person and yet not be able to see him. She was positive someone stood near, almost close enough to touch. She took a deep breath and stepped out firmly in the direction of her own room. The sickly smell went with her.

As she neared her door and reached gratefully for the knob she heard a shuffling footstep behind her and a deep, wheezing breath. So she was right! Linnet turned swiftly and held up her candle, the doorknob under her other hand. A shadowy figure lumbered by her, brushing her nightgown as it passed. Linnet stepped back, uttering a frightened gasp, and the figure padded away into the dark regions at the head of the main staircase. The pervasive scent faded and disappeared.

Violets, that was it! The sweet odour that had haunted her was that of full-blown violets. But there were no violets about the house. Linnet felt instinctively towards her shoulder. Her own bunch of violets which she had bought at the theatre door had disappeared long ago, fallen into the mud no doubt, at the time of her struggle with Otto. Then whence came their scent? It must be perfume. But surely it had not been a woman who had watched her furtively in the darkness out there? And who ever heard of a man who wore perfume?

In any event, whoever it was seemed to have the intention only of watching her, not of harming her. He had come closer, too close for comfort, as she stood by the tower staircase. Was his mission simply to prevent her going up there, for fear of what she might discover? Linnet's fear now was superseded by curiosity. What was there in the tower that she should not find? Something which would prove her true identity, perhaps, or the reason for her strange abduction?

She must get into the tower by some means and discover what it was. She could be mistaken, of course, and find that there was nothing, but Linnet remembered the cry in the night. That too had seemed to originate from the direction of the tower. By some means or other she must get up there and try to solve at least part of the riddle.

But not tonight. Even Linnet's determination was daunted at the prospect of investigating this strange old house at the witching hour, when unperceived eyes followed her everywhere. In the morning, perhaps, if the tower door was still unlocked—then would be her opportunity to slip upstairs.

Despite her warm dressing-gown, Linnet shivered. She had best get back into the warmth of the big old bed before she caught a chill, for the night air was damp and chilly. Then she noticed that the window sash was slightly open, causing a draught in the room.

Linnet put down the candle and crossed to the window. She pushed up the heavy window and looked out into the night, seeing nothing through the heavy mist that enveloped the house. It was almost as if nothing existed outside the solid old building, like a fantasy world where only the tangible objects one could actually touch were real and all the rest was a dream. A dream. Yes, thought Linnet, the whole experience of being here in Willerby Manor with so much left unexplained, had the strange gossamer unreality of a dream. Would she waken in the morning to the shrill clanging of an alarm bell in the Academy and find that this place was but a figment of her overtired imagination, a nightmare brought on by Madame's persecution?

The clammy windowsill felt solid enough beneath her fingertips. Linnet sighed and decided it was time to put an end to such pointless musings and get back into bed. But before she could turn from the window the light appeared again.

Linnet caught her breath. A tiny flame glimmered low at the right of the window and danced its way across to the left and disappeared. It was there, very small but very real. So she had not imagined it the first time after all. What was it? Not a candle carried by someone on the terrace balcony outside, for the breeze would have doused it, and surely too small a flame for a lantern.

She pushed up the lower sash of the window and leaned out, feeling the clammy, damp air on her skin. No sign of the light could be seen on the terrace now, but suddenly, below in the garden, she caught sight of it again, minute and faint now, but still dancing its way into the distance until it disappeared.

Linnet was intrigued, but her eyes were growing heavy with the desire for sleep. She closed the window and drew the curtain. She climbed back into bed, blowing out the candle and snuggling down between the sheets. The old house was full of mystery. Somehow she must get to the bottom of it—but tomorrow, not tonight.

Cissie brought in early-morning tea and drew back the curtains, letting in a watery stream of winter sunlight. Linnet rubbed her eyes and sat up. She watched Cissie pour the amber liquid into a china cup and add the cream, and went over in her mind the events of the previous night. It might be worth while asking Cissie what she knew, for the girl was obviously of a garrulous nature although she had been sworn to silence.

Linnet began by mentioning the light casually as she sipped the hot liquid.

"Light?" repeated Cissie, wide-eyed. "Dunno about that, I'm sure. Like I said, Miss, I don't sleep here at the Manor. I go home down to the village."

"A small light that dances and flickers," Linnet persisted, without much hope of enlightenment, but she felt she must exhaust every possibility with the one person who would talk to her when pressed.

Cissie looked up from the hearth, pausing to wipe an ash-stained hand across her brow. "A light that flickers, Miss? That sounds like a will-o'-the-wisp. Lots of people see them about here, 'cause of the marshes, you know."

She returned to busying herself with the hearth brush. Linnet sat forward, hunching her knees under the bedclothes.

"Will-o'-the-wisp? What's that, Cissie? I've heard of them, but what are they? Is it possible I could have seen one down below, and up here on the balcony too?"

Cissie paused again and considered. "I don't rightly know, Miss," she said uncertainly. "I know I've sometimes seen a light flicker over the marshes when I've been going home late at night, but all I know is as folks call it a will-o'-the-wisp, or a Jack-o'-the-lantern sometimes. But I don't know what it is, really. I don't stop to find out."

"Why not, Cissie?"

" 'Cause they say if you follow it, it'll lead you right into the marsh. They say it's an evil thing, trying to lure you into the deepest part so you can't get out. And them marshes are tricky things. If you don't stick to the path you know, you could soon end up in trouble."

"It's dangerous, is it?"

"Not half it ain't, Miss. Round here it's said to be the most treacherous in all Essex." Cissie looked up at Linnet again. "But you must know that, Miss, you having lived here so long? Mrs Price says you know them marshes like the back of your hand, and that's why we're not to let you outside the house."

So they were back to the insoluble problem again. They all believed Linnet had lived here before. It was a useless tack to pursue that one, so Linnet changed the subject back to the light.

"But I wouldn't see a will-o'-the-wisp up here on the balcony, would I, Cissie?"

"Doubt it, Miss. Far as I know, they're only on the marshes. But if I were you, I wouldn't try to see 'em anyway. Some folks call 'em corpsecandles, and reckon as it's bad luck to see 'em 'cause it means a death. I'd forget all about it, if I were you."

Cissie stood up, brushing down her apron and satisfied that the hearth was now as clean as it should be. Then she picked up the tray and made for the door. Linnet feared that the girl would leave before she had gleaned any more information from her. She flung her last question quickly before she could go.

"Cissie—what is up the tower?"

Cissie looked at her quickly, and Linnet thought her face looked a trifle paler. "Which tower, Miss? There's four."

"The one with the staircase at the end of this corridor."

Cissie was pale. "That's the West Tower," she said in a low voice. "There's nothing there."

"How do you know? Have you been up there?"

"No, Miss. Mrs Price says it's not used, 'cause of the old story about it. No one likes it any more, so it's left empty and unused. Now I've got to get back to the kitchen, Miss, so if you'll please excuse me."

"One moment more, Cissie." The girl hovered in the doorway, anxious to be gone. "Tell me what you know about the tower, however little it is."

"Like I said, Miss, I know nothing 'cept the old story makes people afeard of it, and everyone stays away from the place. Mrs Price told me to keep well clear of it if I valued my life, and anyway it's always locked up."

"The story—what is the story, Cissie?"

Cissie looked fearful. "They say there's a ghost up there, Miss. The ghost of a woman what they walled up on account of she was a wicked woman. I seem to remember Mrs Price told me she was unfaithful to her husband or something—yes, that was it, he found out about it and bricked her up in a wall till she died. An ancestor of yours, she'd be, Miss, one of the Grey family hundreds of years ago."

Linnet listened and reflected. The ghost of a woman walled up many long years ago—was it she who cried so plaintively in the night? Linnet shivered.

"Have you ever heard any sound coming from the tower, Cissie, or of anyone else hearing a cry?"

Cissie started, almost dropping the tea-tray. "Hear it, Miss? No, not me! They say if you ever hear her cry out, you're doomed! I don't want to hear it! Here —" She paused, a flicker of fear and suspicion crossing her pallid face. "You haven't heard anythink, have you, Miss?"

Linnet hesitated. "Well, yes, I think I did hear a cry,

91

like someone in trouble, last night. But I don't know that it came from the tower."

"I hope for your sake as it didn't, Miss." Cissie retreated, her eyes still wide with fear.

Linnet shrugged and began to wash and dress. Really, the whole matter grew preposterously more complicated as time went on. She really must get to the bottom of it soon. And the obvious person to begin to question was the surly, domineering Mr Bellamy. If only he would outgrow his obstinate silence quickly and speak. But he had said he would send for her only when he was ready, and he was obviously a man of stubborn determination, not accustomed to being forced. He would speak, but in his time. Until then she must be patient, or at least try to discover what she could on her own.

After a solitary breakfast in the dining-room, Linnet debated what to do. She was free to roam the whole house, it seemed, with the exception of the tower, for no one ever barred her way. Well, she reasoned with herself, why not descend to the lower regions, to the kitchens, and see whether she could persuade the formidable Mrs Price to let slip some crumb of information which might help her unravel the mystery. It was highly unlikely, but it was at least a line of action. Better than roaming listlessly about.

Linnet felt again the shiver of half-recognition as she crossed the vestibule. What was it about Willerby Manor that seemed so familiar, like a snatch of music that brought back a half-evoked memory? The thought fled as she pushed open the heavy baize-covered door and went down the wide, shallow steps to the servants' quarters. Inwardly she debated how to tackle Mrs Price. Innocent query seemed only to rouse the housekeeper's scorn. Demand then, that might be a better attitude to adopt, for the woman was accustomed to the orders and demands of her superiors.

Mrs Price was coming out of a pantry and hastening along the flagstoned corridor towards the kitchen when she caught sight of Linnet, and she stopped and eyed her quizzically.

"Well, what brings you down here, Miss Grey?" she demanded sharply. Odd, thought Linnet. She speaks to me more as if she were the superior and I but an errant child. She discarded the idea of ordering the woman peremptorily to reveal what she knew. The veiled, suspicious look in the older woman's hooded eyes made it apparent that such a line of approach would not work at all.

"I was just curious to see the kitchens," Linnet replied lamely. Mrs Price snorted.

"You've seen them often enough before, and nothing's changed. We could do with a new stove and plenty more, but you saw to it that we didn't get them. A mind for yourself alone, that's you. No one else ever matters to you, do they, Miss Grey?"

The eyes narrowed and flashed maliciously. Linnet felt resentment rising inside her. "What do you mean by that, Mrs Price? I've never harmed you, nor anyone else, for I tell you I don't know you and, despite your argument, you don't know me either. There obviously has been some mistake."

"Mistake!" The woman spat out the word like a

distasteful pill. She walked ahead of Linnet into the large, flag-floored kitchen and set down on the deal table the tins she was carrying. Then she turned, and her eyes were full of hate. "There's no mistake, Miss Grey. I know you better than most and I have cause to remember you and all your wickedness after what you did to me. I'll remember your vicious spite to the end of my days."

She turned away sharply and began to clatter the tins. Linnet watched her in bewilderment. Then another puzzling feature about the kitchen caught her attention. She frowned for a moment. Yes, there it was—lingering faintly behind the odour of roasting meat in the oven was the cloying sweet smell she remembered. The violets! Was it Mrs Price, then, who had watched her silently in the night? This time she spoke to the housekeeper firmly.

"Mrs Price—what is that scent of violets I can smell?"

The effect of her question on the woman was startling. Mrs Price dropped the tins from her hands on to the table and stared at Linnet with wide and baleful eyes. "Violets—why? Now look here, Miss Grey. I don't want any more trouble with you. Leave me alone! Haven't you done enough? Haven't you caused enough misery in this house? For the Lord's sake, leave us be!"

Linnet stared at her in amazement. There was misery in the woman's face, but it didn't make sense. It was they who had brought Linnet here, and yet Mrs Price was now asking her to leave them alone. It made no sense at all, and Linnet was left speechless. She turned to go, filled with a sense of futile numbness.

The old woman's words, muttered though they were, reached Linnet's ears as she went out of the door. "Doomed, like all the Greys. You'll bring naught but grief and misery to those about you. I know to my cost and it'll be his turn soon, I have no doubt of it. A waste of time, trying to help the likes of you. He'll pay, like all the others, Mr Bellamy will. And you'll squeeze the last drop of life out of him to satisfy your greed, you—vampire."

EIGHT

Mrs Price's hate-filled mutters pursued Linnet along the kitchen corridor and up the stairs. Such venom, so sincerely uttered, could only be based on some terrible, sinister fact of which Linnet had no knowledge. Or had she? Had she, in fact, done some frightful harm to Mrs Price that her mind had then pushed away and refused to remember? Was it possible that the accusations of Bellamy and the housekeeper were true—that Linnet *had* lived in the Manor before?

It was a horrifying thought and Linnet could scarcely bring herself to believe it, but surely the old woman's scorn and hatred of her were real. Unless the old woman was the crazy one. But why, then, had Bellamy had Linnet kidnapped and brought here forcibly? Still it made no sense.

Cissie was scuttling around agitatedly in the vestibule. She straightened the crooked white cap on her head and bobbed a curtsey when she saw Linnet emerging from the baize door.

"Ah, Miss, there you are." Her relief was plainly visible. "The master bid me send you to him in the library, and I couldn't find you anywhere."

"I was below with Mrs Price in the kitchen. I'll go

to Mr Bellamy now," Linnet assured her, and the girl nodded gratefully and disappeared upstairs. Indeed I'll go to Mr Bellamy, thought Linnet decisively. I have no blot on my conscience, I'll face him squarely and have this matter out with him. Her knees shook a little as she approached the library door. Linnet exhorted herself firmly to be brave. After all, the innocent have nothing to fear, she told herself. Linnet knocked and waited for the curt order. "Enter," a voice commanded. Bellamy's stern, unsmiling face across the desk made her quail again.

"Come in," he said coolly. "Please sit." He indicated a horsehair chair near the window, and Linnet sat, her hands dutifully folded in her lap, and waited for him to begin. This was the way it had always been in her life—her presence was commanded and then she waited for orders. Bellamy regarded her thoughtfully, tapping his fingers together, and the room was heavy with silence. Linnet waited, but still he continued to sit and watch and ponder.

He was a handsome man, she reflected; there was no doubt of that. His dark eyes, surmounted by level black brows, had a stern uncompromising honesty about them, and his mouth was generous though firm. This was a lawyer one would instinctively trust if one were his client. He continued to gaze at her fixedly. Linnet's eyes shifted from his sombre face to the tall bookshelves behind him, and then on to the heavy, ornate furniture in the room. It was a beautiful room, the books old and leather-backed and uniform, the side tables and chairs heavy and bulbous and smacking of a bygone age. Then her gaze reverted to the handsome, dour face of the man before her. He wore the patriarchal, commanding look of a man advanced in years and position, but surely he could not yet have reached forty, Linnet mused. How could a man yet young become so severe and solemn?

He cleared his throat and leaned back in his chair. "Miss Grey," he said, and his voice was strong and vibrant, "we must understand each other well, you and I. This time there must be no misunderstanding between us."

"I should indeed be grateful if the situation could be clarified," Linnet admitted.

"Be silent. I shall speak to you, but I would prefer that you do not reply. Thus we shall be spared argument."

Linnet blinked. Very well, let him explain. The sooner he could account for his actions, the better. He was still looking at her curiously.

"I cannot yet determine," he went on eventually, "whether the seeming change in you since last we met is real or feigned. In the last two days you have behaved with calm and decorum, but whether you have truly matured at last or whether you are still trying to gull me, I cannot tell."

Linnet listened in silence. She was waiting for words which made sense, for so far she had followed nothing of what he was saying.

"But let us assume for the moment that you are in earnest. In the two years that have elapsed since you left here, I have done the best I could to safeguard your interests, but the time is fast approaching when you must take over the reins here and manage Willerby yourself."

Linnet's mouth was agape. He was talking utter rubbish now. Was he crazy too, like Mrs Price?

"In only three weeks Willerby becomes legally your property," he went on drily. "There are forms to sign and arrangements to be made. That is why I brought you home. I would have done so sooner, but you covered your tracks well. I must congratulate you on your cleverness, but duty must be done, Miss Grey. None of us can shirk it, not even you."

Linnet could bear no more. She sprang to her feet. "Mr Bellamy, please stop, I entreat you! Please, I beg you, explain to me what is going on. None of what you are saying makes sense to me at all. You say I left here two years ago—but I have never been in this house in my life before, I swear it!"

She stood before his desk, her hands outstretched in pleading, but Bellamy's face remained set and impassive.

"Sit down again, Miss Grey. Nothing can be gained from histrionics. I am unmoved by your act, though I bow to your talent. Let us simply settle the details of your inheritance, and when my duty to your father is discharged, I can leave here. Then, and only then, the estate is yours and you can do with it as you will. But I must first fulfil the pledge I made to your father."

Linnet sat down, limp and dejected. Nothing she said seemed to penetrate his determination to go on believing she was other than she was. His words drifted to her ears through a haze of bewilderment.

"As you know, you will come of age in three weeks' time and Willerby Manor, up to now held in trust for you, will pass to you. Then I, whom your father charged to manage the estate and his money until this time, can be relieved of my burden."

Come of age? Linnet was perplexed. It would be more than two years yet before she reached twenty-one. And her father? He had no manor, she was sure, for he spent all his life away at sea. So what was Bellamy's game? He surely could not be trying to force on to her an estate to which she had no legitimate claim. Linnet's head began to throb with confusion.

"Believe me, I had no personal desire to drag you back here," Bellamy went on. "But for the legal matter I would gladly have left you in London, for life was far more peaceful here without you and your mischief-making. But I promised your father before he died, leaving you motherless and alone, that I would care for you, and I tried. Even when you ran away I tried for months to trace you, but I finally had to give in, for you took great care to conceal yourself well. But for your sudden rise to fame, I should probably not have found you at all."

Fame? What did he mean? Linnet gave up trying to follow his meaning, for her head was throbbing now fiercely with the effort.

"Let me render account to you for what I have done in your absence," Bellamy said. "I gave orders for the rebuilding of the coach-house, for it was on the verge of collapse, and can give you detailed figures for the cost of materials and labour. You had expressly forbidden improvements in the kitchens, so

103

I obeyed your will, much to Mrs Price's disappointment. So you will no doubt find that expense will shortly be necessay in that quarter. Itemised accounts for the servants' wages you will find in detail in this ledger." He pushed a thick account book across the desk towards her, but Linnet made no move. "Costs for coal, food, cleaning materials and so on I have listed separately. Will you see them?"

Linnet closed her eyes and shook her head slowly. "No, no more. Do as you will, Mr Bellamy, for I can take no more."

She passed a weary hand across her brow. Bellamy rose and came round the desk to her, a sardonic smile on his lips.

"You still have no interest in the running of the estate, it seems, Miss Grey. But before long you must control it alone, for I shall soon be free to leave. You must make an effort to take an interest, for your own sake."

Linnet rose and made for the door. It was all too much for her. She was living through a fantastic nightmare that became more and more incomprehensible at every step. At the doorway she turned and made a last, desperate effort to reach for sanity.

"Mr Bellamy, I have not understood a word of what you have been saying tonight, nor why I am here. My name is Linnet Grey. I am eighteen and a teacher. My parents are both dead and I have never been in Willerby Manor in my life until this week. Somewhere, somehow, there has been a ghastly mistake and I beg you to clarify it and return me to London so that I can continue my life, humdrum though it may have been. Please, Mr Bellamy, help me or I fear I may go mad."

Bellamy was leaning on the desk, the glow of the lamp behind surrounding his tall, lean frame. He listened in silence, then straightened up and came across to her, resting his hand on her shoulder.

"Take my advice, my dear," he said softly. "Do not fight destiny. Willerby is your destiny, as it has been for the Greys for generations. It is useless to act, to pretend you are what you are not. You must accept what life offers you—and that includes the duties and responsibilities too. I admit, your sincere-seeming act just now would have taken in many, but not me, my child, not any more. I know you for the shallow, selfish creature you are, and had hoped that two years struggling alone would have improved you. Don't disappoint me. Don't try to forget who you are, hiding behind the façade of the irresponsible person you would like to be. It takes courage, but the Greys were ever a courageous family. After all, you will be twenty-one very soon now. Rise to the challenge, accept the role of responsibility, and everyone will admire you the more for it."

Linnet choked and turned and fled to her room. It was useless. Despite her appeal, he was confusing her even more, and the pain in her forehead was intense.

She lay on her bed, her head throbbing, and ignored the bell that summoned her to lunch. After a time Cissie peered round the door to remind her that lunch was laid, and Mr Bellamy required to know the reason for her non-appearance at the table.

"I am not well," Linnet moaned. "Pray tell Mr Bellamy I am indisposed and shall not be taking lunch today."

"Shall I bring you up a tray then, Miss?"

"Don't bother, Cissie. I am not hungry."

Cissie looked flustered. "But Mr Bellamy is expecting company this evening, Miss. He won't like it if the day's routine is disturbed."

"Company?" Linnet repeated laconically. She was really too tired and confused to summon up much interest, but company at this desolate, deserted house did seem unusual.

"Yes, Miss. Friend of Mr Bellamy's, Mrs Price says. A Mr Rupert, from London. Shall I say you'll be down to dinner with them this evening then, Miss?"

"In all probability, Cissie. Now please leave me, for I have a fearful headache."

Cissie looked concerned. "Then let me bring you a cold compress, Miss, or somethink. A nice cup of tea, eh?"

Linnet shook her head, slowly and painfully. "Thank you, but no. Just leave me to rest, there's a good girl."

Cissie nodded understandingly and withdrew. Linnet lay on the bed, staring at the high carved ceiling above and willing the pain in her temples to abate. It was no good. The more she went over in her mind Bellamy's cryptic words the more confused and unintelligible it became. There must have been a mistake. He must have confused her with someone else—but whom?

Something filtered through Linnet's foggy torpor

and caused her mind to bridle with alarm. She sat upright. What was it? Some sixth sense seemed to warn her of danger—but what? Linnet sat tense, straining every nerve to listen and watch. There was nothing to see or to hear, but still something jangled. The smell! That was it! A faint, almost undetectable odour of violets lingered in the air, practically imperceptible, but to Linnet's taut senses undeniably there. Linnet slithered from the bed and looked about the room. No one was hiding there, nor was there a scent of violets among the bed linen or in the clothes in the vast wardrobe. She lifted her head high and sniffed again. Yes, it was still there, faint but menacing. Had someone furtively opened the door while she dozed and spied on her?

Linnet wrenched the door open, but the corridor outside was deserted. Nor was there any trace of the malicious scent out there. She closed the door and recrossed the room. By the fireplace she stopped suddenly. Here, yes here, the scent was strongest.

Linnet searched feverishly around the fireplace, but the smell seemed to linger in the air about it without having any source. It was most puzzling. Eventually, Linnet had to admit defeat and cease searching. But still the menacing air remained and Linnet sensed again that she was being watched. Here, in her own room? It was impossible. The door was heavy and solid, and the only window looked out over the garden. There was the narrow balcony, of course, but Linnet made sure that no one was out there looking in.

She must have dozed off at last, for the next thing she knew she was awakened by a light tap at the door. Cissie came in and bobbed.

"The master's compliments, Miss, and he begs you will favour himself and Mr Rupert with your company at dinner."

Linnet leapt up, all trace of her headache gone. "Is it time for dinner already, Cissie?" She must have slept long and deeply, she reflected.

"Not yet, Miss, but Mr Bellamy wanted me to give you good warning. He bid me say as he'd like you to dress specially for the guest and be on your most charming behaviour like he says you know well how to do if you've a mind to it. As a special favour to him, he says."

Linnet snorted. Why should Bellamy presume to ask a favour of her, after his startlingly odd behaviour towards her? Nevertheless, she dismissed Cissie, saying she would be down shortly, and began to prepare. She selected a beautiful deep-green velvet gown from the closet, not too décolletée, and brushed her smooth hair till it glistened before binding it carefully. A few drops of the toilet water from the bottle on the dressing-table, and she was ready. She took a final, appraising glance in the pier-glass. Yes, the effect was pleasing. Mr Bellamy could not be disapproving of her well-turned-out but demure appearance.

There was no one about downstairs in the vestibule, and Linnet decided that as the gong had not yet rung for dinner she might as well take a walk in the conservatory. Again she had that strange, intangible sense of familiarity with the place as she crossed to the garden-room door. It was odd, but somehow no longer frightening. In fact, it was almost a peaceful, reassuring feeling.

The conservatory was still and heavy, redolent with the scent of many blooms. It was stiflingly warm, and Linnet realised it must be kept heated on account of the tropical plants which flourished there. She wandered among the thick foliage, breathing in deeply the humid, powerfully-scented air. A huge red bloom caught her eye, and Linnet pulled the lush flower gently down to smell it. As she did so, she heard a cough, gentle but discreet, from the far side of the densely-leaved plant. She stepped back, startled, for she had believed herself alone.

"I beg your pardon, Madame, I did not mean to startle you." A light, concerned voice came from beyond the bush, followed almost simultaneously by the wide-eyed face of a young man. He was tall and sandy-haired, and his look registered genuine concern. "I fear I broke in upon your musings," the light voice continued. "Forgive me if I alarmed you."

Linnet smiled. She was relieved that this time she was not being secretly watched, and she was anxious to put the young man at his ease.

"You must be Mr Rupert, Mr Bellamy's guest," she said warmly. "I fear I do not know your full name."

"Rupert Manning, ma'am, at your service." He bowed, a stiff, formal bow, and straightened again. His face showed only pleasure at the sight of her, and Linnet warmed to him. He was the first to show her a

109

friendly countenance since she had come to this place, and she would be glad of friendship. Perhaps he could be of help to her.

He was watching her with an anticipatory look now. Linnet realised he was waiting for her to introduce herself. She hesitated for a moment, and he prompted her.

"And you? You must be Marcus's ward of whom I have heard so much, are you not?"

"Indeed I am not." The words slipped out hotly and involuntarily. Rupert Manning's eyebrows rose.

"Not Miss Grey? Then with whom, may I ask, have I the pleasure of conversing?"

"My name is—Miss Linnet." Her voice faltered and died. She could not bring herself to say her surname, since he had said he knew of Miss Grey.

The young man was smiling broadly. "Miss Linnet," he repeated slowly, savouring the words, "I am indeed delighted to make your acquaintance, but I wonder why Marcus did not tell me we were to have such a ravishing fourth to dinner. He told me only that his ward, Miss Grey, would be here. Perhaps he intended to surprise me, and indeed, it is a most delightful surprise."

Linnet smiled shyly. In her way of life she had not been accustomed to receiving compliments from handsome young gentlemen, and she was uncertain how to handle such compliments gracefully. She seated herself on the wrought-iron bench that Rupert had lately occupied, and indicated to him to sit beside her. He swept up his coat tails and did so with alacrity. Then he sighed and stretched in contentment.

"You cannot tell, Miss Linnet, what a relief it was to me to discover you were not Miss Grey, for I really felt quite dismayed."

"Dismayed, Mr Manning? But why? Do you not know the lady?"

"In person, no, but her reputation is widespread."

"What do you know of her, pray?"

"Very little, really, beyond what Marcus tells me. But do you not know her?"

"Not at all." It was the truth, she reflected, and she was anxious to hear what Rupert Manning knew. "What does Marcus say of her?"

Rupert laughed. "Only that she is one of the wickedest, most selfish creatures that the good Lord ever created, and he would to blazes he could be rid of her."

NINE

Linnet was convinced that it was no mere accident that caused the dinner gong to sound at that very moment, but a deliberate and malicious stroke on someone's part to prevent her learning more from this lighthearted young Rupert Manning about Marcus's relationship with the mysterious Miss Grey. Not herself, of course, but the cryptical alter ego they all appeared to mistake her for, the wilful, wild and capricious Miss Grey who was so soon to inherit Willerby Manor.

Rupert was standing watching her. The silence was permeated only by the rhythmic tinkling of a fountain, and the air was heavy with the scent of the tropical plants. Rupert held out his hand. "Shall we go in to dinner, Miss Linnet? I had not realised it was so late, for I had planned to join Marcus in the study before the gong sounded."

"Yes, indeed, let us go in." Linnet took the proffered arm and went into the house with him. He was a courteous, charming young man, and Linnet had need of a friend, an ally even. He radiated warmth and friendliness.

Marcus was standing by the head of the dinner

table. His fine dark eyebrows rose at the sight of Rupert and Linnet arm in arm.

"I wondered where you were, Rupert. I see you two have already met, so introductions now would seem a trifle unnecessary. Will you sit here, my dear?"

He was addressing Linnet, who took the chair he pulled out for her. The table was laid for three, and Linnet noticed Rupert's eyebrows rise in query, but he said nothing. Instead, he seated himself on the other side of her, and he and Marcus began to chat easily and warmly as old friends do. It was then that Linnet saw for the first time how Marcus's face took on a new light, a radiance, and the stern tightness faded as he talked. He had an air of exuberance and vitality that showed he was a man of youthful vigour, and not the dry, taciturn, ageing stick she had taken him for. And although his talk was directed mainly at Rupert, he did not neglect to treat Linnet courteously, passing her dishes with deft quick fingers and a warm smile, and Linnet began to wonder whether her senses were betraying her again. How could a man switch so suddenly from dictatorial sternness to warm friendliness? Was it all part of a calculated plan to confuse her yet further, so that she no longer knew whether she was on her head or her heels, sane or crazy?

If so, she resolved inwardly, his plan was not going to work. She would cling on tenaciously to the knowledge of who she was, Linnet Grey, orphan and schoolteacher. As yet she did not know what his plan might be, but she would find out, and thwart it if she could.

Rupert Manning was smiling at her across the candles, twirling his brandy glass between his fingers. Yes, with his help she would find out what lay at the bottom of all this mystery. Friend of Marcus Bellamy or no, she was certain Rupert was not the kind of man to ignore the pleas of a maid in distress.

Marcus was pouring a liberal helping of brandy for himself now. Linnet rose and made to leave.

"I shall withdraw and leave you gentlemen to enjoy your brandy in peace," she said. Even if she were not born of the higher classes, she knew enough of the proprieties to know this was the done thing.

"I entreat you, do not go." Marcus's deep voice startled Linnet. "Do not leave us, my dear, for all beauty leaves the room when you go."

Linnet sat down again in stunned silence. A compliment from Marcus was the last thing she had expected, especially as he seemed to be a man who did not make such remarks lightly. Some reply seemed to be expected of her. Linnet searched for something suitable to say. Unthinkingly, she spoke as a guest.

"It seems to me, Mr Bellamy, that beauty could not leave this room unless you were to strip it, for in my life I have never seen a room so elegantly designed and decorated. It was a person of taste indeed who planned and executed your dining-room."

Rupert was nodding in agreement. "Indeed, Marcus. Such tasteful hangings and furniture and such fine silver. Such a dining-room calls for frequent dinner parties and fun, don't you think?"

Marcus was surveying Linnet with a puzzled frown as he answered. "Yes, indeed, Rupert. The whole house clamours for company and happy living. It has been a lonely house too long."

Rupert leaned forward over the table. "Yes—I have that feeling about the place too," he said eagerly. "It's a beautiful house, but it has a strange, unhappy air of neglect about it."

"You are sensitive to atmosphere, I see," Marcus commented drily.

"Aren't we all? I'm sure Miss Linnet is too. Don't you feel the unhappiness here? Has the house perhaps a sad history, Marcus?"

Marcus shrugged. "I think possibly every house retains some of the emotion of the people who have lived in it, and not all events have been happy ones."

Rupert banged his glass down. "Then I think it time the sadness were exorcised. Parties, dinners, balls—that's what Willerby Manor needs, don't you agree, Marcus? I love parties. When can we start?"

Marcus turned to Linnet. "Do you mind if I smoke, my dear?"

Linnet shook her head. Marcus drew a pipe and pouch from his pocket and began to fill the pipe slowly and leisurely. Rupert watched him impatiently.

"Well? What do you say?"

Marcus rammed the tobacco home deliberately. "It is not for me to say, my friend. As you know, I am but the curator, as you might say. But in a few weeks my ward, Miss Grey, may make whatever decisions she will as to Willerby Manor. You must discuss your scheme with her, my friend."

Linnet hung her head in embarrassment. Now it

would come out. Now Marcus would say she was this Miss Grey, and her new-found friend would be lost to her. Gone now were her dreams of an ally.

Marcus rose and crossed to the fireplace, took a taper from a jar on the mantelshelf, and lit it from the fire. He stood there puffing on his pipe until it was well alight. Rupert pushed his chair back from the table.

"And so I will, Marcus. But tomorrow, not tonight. Would you come for a stroll on the terrace before bed, Miss Linnet? I find the fumes of Marcus's pipe unbearable."

Linnet hesitated, her eyes on Marcus. She would dearly love to get out on to the terrace, damp and chilly though the night was, for the old house was becoming claustrophobic to her. But would Marcus permit her to go beyond the door, accompanied only by someone who was apparently not in his plot?

Marcus looked up from his pipe. "Do go, my dear, but bid Cissie fetch your wrap first, for it is treacherously damp out there."

Linnet rose, feeling cross with him for his feigned concern. But he did pull the bell rope and send a curious Cissie to fetch the wrap. Once outside, Linnet was glad of his warning, for the night air on the terrace was insidiously cold and clammy despite the warmth of Rupert's arm on her elbow, and she pulled the shawl closer about her. But for her devouring curiosity to learn more from Rupert about her host, she would gladly have suggested they delayed their stroll till the morrow.

Rupert's talk made it evident that he still took Linnet for someone other than Marcus's ward, a guest in the manor like himself, and Linnet was greatly relieved. Now was her chance to ask him, as discreetly as she could, what he knew. It was he who eventually gave her the opportunity.

"What a pity the fair Miss Grey did not put in an appearance at dinner tonight," he commented regretfully as they reached the end of the terrace and leaned on the balustrade looking out over the darkened garden. "Perhaps she was indisposed, for I noted the table was set only for the three of us. I wonder that Marcus did not explain her absence. Do you know the reason, Miss Linnet?"

"I fear not, Mr Manning."

"You know the lady, I take it?"

"Not at all. I have never met her." It was no less than the truth, but Linnet was glad of the chance to speak of the mysterious ward. "I know very little about Miss Grey, in fact, though I confess I am curious. Has Marcus spoken often of her to you?"

Linnet blushed at her own temerity. She referred to Bellamy by his Christian name, knowing that it implied a degree of intimacy, of friendship between her and him, and inviting Rupert to discuss Bellamy with her in this light. It betokened the young man's lack of guile that he patently accepted her at once as Bellamy's friend.

"Oh, often," he laughed. "Often he has had cause to air his frustration over the young lady, and as his close friend I have heard much of her."

"Though you do not know her?"

"No. She had recently run away from the Manor

and Marcus's guardianship when he and I met, and he was deeply concerned that he could not trace her."

"But from all Marcus says, it seems he cares little for her. Why, then, was he so concerned?"

Rupert turned and eyed Linnet earnestly. "Marcus is a man of honour and integrity, as you must know, Miss Linnet. He takes his responsibilities very seriously, and especially a duty to such a friend as Thomas Grey had been to him."

"Thomas Grey? Miss Grey's father?"

"That is right. I never knew the old man, of course, but it seems he took Marcus on as a junior partner in his firm—he, too, was a lawyer—but from what I hear he treated Marcus more like a son than a junior employee. As the years passed they grew closer, and Marcus was convinced that the old man took to him in place of the son he never had."

"He had daughters, then?" Linnet prompted when Rupert seemed to be relapsing into his own private thoughts.

"Only one. The celebrated, wilful heiress I expected to meet tonight."

"I wonder he had no more children in that event," Linnet murmured thoughtfully.

"He did not have the opportunity, for his wife died in giving birth to her daughter. Old Thomas was heartbroken, for he adored his beautiful French wife, and he vowed he would never marry again."

"Poor man. No wonder Willerby Manor has such an air of sadness." Linnet felt truly sympathetic for the saddened old man, having to adopt his junior partner in place of a son.

"Sadder than you know," Rupert went on thoughtfully, murmuring as if to himself. "Thomas's childhood had not been a particularly happy one. His parents were probably loving enough, but their love extended only to providing material benefits for their son. They were the cold, undemonstrative kind, and when Thomas's elder brother died tragically . . ."

"He was not an only child, then?"

"Not at first, but his brother was drowned, it seems, in the river here when Thomas was only nine or ten years old. His parents withdrew even more into a shell, of grief no doubt, and his childhood was a lonely one, as you can imagine, in this deserted place."

Rupert was leaning on his elbows on the balustrade, gazing out into the darkness. "And then?" Linnet prompted.

"Oh, well, when he grew older he went away to train as a lawyer, took the opportunity to travel abroad, met a beautiful French girl—I think her name was Estelle—and brought her home as his wife. The old parents died, and Thomas inherited Willerby."

"And he was happy? For a time, at least?"

Rupert shook his head doubtfully. "Not from what Marcus told me. Estelle was gay and lively, and she hated this bleak place. Thomas did his best to make her happy, inviting company to the house and throwing parties, but it was not enough. Estelle wanted to go and live in London, where life had more to offer."

"Then why did Thomas not go to live there? After all, his practice was there, was it not?"

"It all seems so easy to you, does it not, Miss Linnet? No, Thomas realised that Estelle, pretty and

122

lively as she was, was also flighty and thriftless. He thought it wiser to keep her out of the way of London's temptations. But she pined and fretted and became thin and listless."

"Then he should have let her have her way," Linnet retorted. "It was cruel of him!"

Rupert smiled. "It was then that they discovered that Estelle was to have a child, and Thomas promised that she should have all she desired once the child was born. But for the time being he considered that Willerby was a safer place to bear it. He would not have deprived Estelle of her wish for long, for he adored her, petulent and demanding as she was, but it was not to be."

"Because—she died?"

"Yes. The same night as the child was born. Thomas's joy over the birth of his daughter turned to grief in an instant. He was filled with remorse at not having kept his promise to grant Estelle all she desired."

"And so he spoilt his daughter as a result—by way of atonement," Linnet stated in a flash of understanding. "I see it all now."

"Not at first, though. After Estelle's death, he could not bear to see the child at first. But as time passed he grew to love her, for in her ways, if not appearance, she resembled her mother greatly. The same wilful, demanding manner, combined with flashes of sweetness and sunny smiles. Eventually she had Thomas as captive as her mother had done, and all she demanded he gave without question."

"I see," Linnet murmured. Whoever this unknown

Miss Grey was, it was apparent now that her wild, demanding manner was not entirely her own fault. Her well-meaning father who had loved her overmuch had had a lot to do with it.

"And that is how Marcus came into it," Rupert went on. "By the time he was thirty and a respected member of Thomas's firm, he was also a close friend of the old man. Thomas knew he was ill and had not long to live, and asked Marcus to be the executor of his will, to manage his estate until his daughter was of age. Marcus did not care then for the spoilt child, but he could not refuse a dying friend's request."

"But he has come to regret it, I think," Linnet said quietly.

"Not his duty, for he is a man of his word, but he has grown to like his ward less and less, and I think he will be glad to discharge his duty at last and be rid of her and the manor."

"He hates her?" Linnet asked, and was shocked at her own strong words.

"He has not said so openly, but he hints that she has done terrible harm."

"To him?"

"To others, at least. He does not speak of her misdeeds explicitly. But he has called me here today because he says there is still a matter he must decide, and he cannot bring himself to make the decision until he has discussed it objectively with another."

"Do you know what the decision he has to make may be?"

Rupert shook his sandy head. "No, not yet. I am to meet him in his study in the morning and I think I shall learn then. I hope I may be of help to him, for there is not a finer, more honest man than Marcus Bellamy and I would be glad to help to lift a worry from his mind."

Rupert shook himself as if to detach himself from the oppressive tenor of their conversation. "But tell me, Miss Linnet, why are you here in Willerby Manor? Obviously not as a friend of Miss Grey's, so I must assume you are Marcus's friend. Did you not already know of his concerns?"

Linnet hesitated. How could she reply to this question? It would sound ridiculous to say she had been kidnapped and had known nothing of this strange, laconic man Bellamy until tonight. She drew her wrap around her and shivered.

"Oh, Miss Linnet, you are cold! How thoughtless of me!" Rupert exclaimed. "Let us return indoors."

He took her arm and led her towards the door. As they neared it, Bellamy's tall frame was silhouetted in the lighted doorway, broad and challenging.

"Ah, there you are," his vibrant voice came to them in the cook dark. "I was concerned that you were staying overlong out there in the cold. I have sent Cissie to take hot chocolate up to your room, Miss Grey. I think it best you come in out of the treacherous night air quickly."

Linnet cast a last quick look over her shoulder as she brushed past him. Rupert Manning's face was white and aghast in the light of the oil lamp as he watched her run up the stairs.

125

TEN

Linnet's conscience troubled her deeply, for she had not meant to cheat Rupert Manning, but much as she pondered the vexed question, the more she reassured herself staunchly that she had nothing with which to reproach her conscience. She could not, in all truth, have told him she was the Miss Grey they apparently all disliked so intensely, for she was not. Perhaps she should have told him, however, that Bellamy and Mrs Price seemed to be under some spell in that they both mistook her for the wicked creature.

But she had done no more and no less than was asked of her. Bellamy had begged her to be a charming hostess to his guest, and that she had tried to be. Over dinner she had spoken little, but then Bellamy had apparently not expected her to converse, but simply to smile and exude charm.

And what of Bellamy himself? His warmth and charm over dinner had completely taken Linnet by surprise. Hitherto a stern, cold, unapproachable creature, he now appeared in a totally different light, friendly and light-hearted. Was it a measure of the man's duplicity that he could change so quickly and so radically? Linnet warned herself not to be taken in by his apparent charm, but to remember that this was the man who had snatched her violently from her former way of life, and who so far had offered no logical explanation. Why, even if he genuinely mistook her for his ward Miss Grey, was she continually watched? What reason was there for a trustee to spy on a legitimate heiress? And why the menacing air about this house, the ominous scent of violets, and the cries and lights in the night?

It just did not make sense. Linnet was deeply sorry about Rupert Manning, for in him she sensed she could have found a valuable ally. But now, believing her to be a deceitful liar, he would not wish to speak to her again. And if he was Bellamy's friend, he would be sure to take his part in a difference between Bellamy and his supposed ward. Linnet sighed and fell uneasily asleep.

In the morning Linnet rose early, dressed, and went down to breakfast. To her surprise and dismay, Bellamy was already at the table. It was unusual for him to take breakfast in the dining-room, which she usually had to herself. However, she smiled uncertainly and seated herself opposite him.

"Good morning, Mr Bellamy," she said softly, unfolding her napkin and attempting to behave as if all were well and normal, and she were not an abducted girl facing her kidnapper.

"Good morning," Marcus replied crisply, reaching for another slice of toast. He buttered it in silence, and Linnet noted he took care to avoid meeting her gaze.

"Where is Mr Manning this morning? Is he not

coming down to breakfast?" Linnet asked innocently, in an effort to act naturally.

Marcus put down his knife and looked directly at her for the first time. "He is not. He is not anxious to meet you again after last night. Do you blame him?"

Linnet looked at him wide-eyed. "Why not? What did I do that was so reprehensible, may I ask? What sin have I committed?"

Marcus sighed. "If you do not know, then I cannot teach you. There are none so blind as those who will not see."

Linnet began to grow angry. He was acting as if he were the injured party instead of herself. "Now look here, Mr Bellamy," she said firmly, leaning across the table to stare directly into those dark, uncompromising eyes. "I have done nothing, absolutely nothing, of which I should feel ashamed. On the contrary, it is you, who brought me here forcibly and against my will, who should search your own conscience. I feel it is you who owe me an explanation and apology, and some attempt at making amends for what you have done."

She sat back, full of righteous indignation. How dare he adopt an attitude of fatherly patience and forbearance towards her, and he the sinner all the time! Marcus was staring at her.

"I—apologise to you—after all the worry and mischief you have caused!" he muttered in a low voice. "That's rich—indeed it is. But I think you overstep the mark, young lady, to dupe my friends as you did Rupert Manning. He is a kindhearted, gullible young fellow, and believed your every word. His shock and dismay is beyond words at discovering your fraudulence."

"But I am no fraud! I am Linnet Grey, not your ward as you would have everyone else and myself believe!" Linnet cried out.

Marcus pursed his lips tightly. "If you choose to turn your back on your past and your inheritance, that is no concern of mine, or at least it will not be so very soon. But in the last remaining days I must try to make you see and understand your responsibility to Willerby. I will not give up the attempt until your birthday has arrived."

"But I tell you, I am *not* your ward!" Linnet could have wept with vexation. A sudden light hit her. "Can you prove that I am? Have you any evidence to verify your mad claim? I am Linnet Grey, teacher at Madame Roland's Academy for Young Ladies, and I defy you to prove that I am not!"

A slow smile crossed Marcus's saturnine countenance. "Linnet—a pretty name," he commented. "Not your given name at birth, but a pretty choice nonetheless. Very well, we shall call you Linnet, if you prefer it."

"Do not humour me! I am Linnet! And there I have you, do I not, for you cannot prove otherwise?"

Marcus was eyeing her soberly during her outburst. "You think not? Then follow me, my dear, and I shall give you the evidence you require." So saying, he pushed back his chair and crossed to the door, where he waited for her, let her pass, then followed out into the corridor. Linnet waited to see what he would do.

He strode away purposefully and Linnet hastened after him. Up the stairs and along a corridor she followed quickly, and at the door of a bedroom he paused. "Wait here."

He went in, and from the doorway Linnet recognised the stark, masculine room she had entered on her first day at Willerby Manor. She watched him cross to the locked secretaire by the window, withdraw a bunch of keys from his pocket, select one, and unlock the desk with it.

From this distance Linnet could not discern its contents, but presently Marcus straightened, a bundle of white cards in his hand. He scanned through them briefly and then recrossed the room to join her at the door.

"Here," he said with a hint of a smile, "is the proof you asked for." He placed the cards in Linnet's hand. She saw then that they were a collection of photographs, the sepia-brown tints beginning to fade with age. She peered at each photograph in the dim light in the corridor, but could see little with any clarity, and Marcus obviously noted her difficulty.

"Come," he said curtly, and led the way across the room to the window. Linnet stood by its light and turned over each photo carefully. Each one showed a girl, the same girl, at different ages, and Linnet could scarcely believe her eyes. The girl had a haughty, defiant air about the way she held her head, and a proud, selfish curl to the full lips, but there was an unmistakable familiarity about every picture. It was almost like looking into a mirror. The face was undeniably Linnet's own, though the rich, glossy hair in the later ones was dressed far more fashionably than Linnet's had ever been.

Marcus watched her silently. Linnet turned over the last photo, and her breath was almost taken away. It was of a mature man, grey and handsome, with side whiskers and a gentle smile, and it was her own father to the life, though older and plumper than she remembered him. Moreover, in the picture he wore a waistcoat with a gold chain extending across his stomach, not the trim naval uniform he always wore in her memory. But it was undoubtedly he—or his twin.

Linnet's heart thudded and threatened to stop altogether. Was she going crazy? How could Marcus Bellamy possibly have photographs of herself and her father in his keeping unless his wild story was true? She stared at Bellamy thunderstruck, the photographs held out limply in her hand.

"You recognise them?" Marcus demanded. "All photographs of yourself as a child and up to the time you left here two years ago, with the exception of one —the photograph of your father. You recognise him?"

"I—I think so," Linnet admitted weakly.

"Of course you do. Who could forget so kindly a man as Thomas Grey?" Marcus's voice was gentler as it lingered on the name. Linnet bridled.

"But while I remember his face, I also remember his name, Mr Bellamy. My father's name was not Thomas, but Robert. Robert Grey, captain of the Queen's Navy."

Marcus was returning the bundle of photographs to the pigeonhole in his secretaire. At her words he

134

looked up sharply. "What are you saying? Is this another instance of your malicious nature, young lady?" He came to look her full in the face.

"Indeed no! My father's name was Robert, and my mother was named Caroline. I remember them both well—you cannot cheat me so easily."

"I—cheat you! It is you, my girl, who are now trying to confuse matters again. It is my guess that you heard of your father's dead brother, young Robert, and you are using his tragic death to your ends."

"But I tell you my father was named Robert Grey!" Linnet was near to tears now. "Probably not the Robert you refer to, but it was his name nonetheless. Oh, I wish I could convince you, Mr Bellamy, that I am not who you think I am. Whatever has led you to believe otherwise, I cannot tell, but I wish you would believe me and allow me to go back to London."

"I am sure you wish to return to London, for you struggled long before you escaped there the last time, but I am not taken in by your story, my dear." Marcus's voice was full of disciplined patience. "As I said, your acting the part of the hurt innocent is excellent and would fool many, but not me. You asked for proof that you were my ward, and I have given it to you. Can you deny that those were photographs of yourself?"

"No," Linnet admitted in a low tone, and tried to prevent him hearing the break in her voice.

"Then let us cease this game of let's-pretend. It does no good to you or to me either. And as for Rupert . . ."

He was taking her arm to lead her out of the room. At the same moment as Linnet became aware of the warm tingle that his touch caused on her arm, she also realised with a start of excitement that he had not re-locked the secretaire. In his distress over the mention of Robert's name, he had forgotten it.

Marcus saw her out, nodded curtly and re-entered the room and closed the door. In the dim corridor Linnet heard footsteps clop-clopping towards her. Mrs Price's face appeared, pale and frowning and seemingly disembodied as her dark dress merged into the gloom of the passage. She granted Linnet only a fleeting, distasteful look before knocking restrainedly on Marcus's door. His voice bade her enter, and Mrs Price disappeared inside.

Linnet began to walk aimlessly back towards the staircase, then paused. If she bided her time and waited hereabouts, perhaps Bellamy would leave his room shortly and then would come her opportunity to slip in. A quick look at the contents of the secretaire might possibly reveal further clues as to the mystery that surrounded this gloomy old house and its heiress. She did not know what she would look for, but any clue would be important in her present state of confusion. There might be something of importance which could contradict the apparent evidence of the photographs.

She crept noiselessly back past Bellamy's door, making for the sanctuary of her own room. Hushed voices were murmuring within, but she could not make out the words. In her own room she sat at the dressing-table and stared at her pale reflection in the mirror. These past few days of being imprisoned indoors had given her cheeks a wan, unhealthy pallor. Oh, for a chance just to go for an invigorating walk in the fresh air!

Suddenly a low, scratching sound came to Linnet's ears. She stiffened and sat upright. The sound ceased, and then seconds later she heard it again. It was coming from the direction of the fireplace. She looked across to it, but about the high, ornately-carved mantelpiece there was nothing to be seen. There it was again! And it seemed to come from above the fireplace this time. Linnet dismissed the idea of mice in the skirting boards, for the sound was from above. Perhaps they were in the wainscoting

She rose and crossed to the fireplace. Now there was absolute silence, undisturbed for the several minutes she stood there. Imagination, or mice, that was all, she decided. But then suddenly her nose caught the scent again, the scent she had come to dread, the menace of the violets. Linnet shuddered. How could the malodorous perfume haunt her everywhere she went?

Linnet pulled herself together. It was no use cowering, like a shrinking violet herself. She must investigate. Purposefully she pulled a heavy chair to the hearth and stood up on it. It was a good job Cissie had not lit the fire here today yet, or the hem of Linnet's frock would have been endangered.

The mantelshelf was innocent of all nooks and crannies, so far as she could see. The wall rising to the ceiling above was of moulded plaster, shaped to form patterns and little figures of nymphs and goddesses, and Linnet's fingers probed the curves. After a mo-

137

ment or two she looked at her blackened fingertips distastefully. She was gaining nothing but dirty hands from this venture, and she was about to climb down again when she noticed a dark hollow in one of the moulded curves. She reached up and poked her finger in, and to her surprise her finger disappeared straight through the hole, and she could feel cool air beyond. So that was it! A peephole in the wall above the high mantelshelf! A hole which made her the easy victim to any prying eye!

But whose eye? Who had made the scuffling noise only a few minutes ago? Someone had been surveying her then, she knew it. Small wonder she had had the uncanny feeling she was being watched ever since she came to this house. What was the spy hoping to see? Something in her manner which would betray the fact that she really was the malicious heiress, perhaps?

But no more. Linnet climbed down off the chair and made purposefully for Marcus Bellamy's room. She would tell him she knew of the peephole and wanted no more of this. How disgraceful! How could a man like Marcus Bellamy, supposedly so rigid and honourable, condone anyone's spying on a defenceless girl?

Cissie was standing, half-crouched, outside Bellamy's door. She straightened guiltily and flushed when she saw Linnet.

"Oh, Miss—I didn't mean to eavesdrop, but I heard 'em talking, Mrs Price and the master—about you, Miss."

Linnet smiled. There was no malice in the child,

however stupid she was. "That's all right, Cissie. You may go."

Cissie scuttled away and Linnet paused. What could Mrs Price have to say to Bellamy about herself? She was curious, and, making sure that no one was about, she adopted Cissie's recent attitude near the door, half-crouched to the keyhole. Maybe it was not honest, nor polite even, but if they were discussing herself, then she had every right to hear, she argued with her conscience.

The voices were low and indiscernible. Suddenly Mrs Price's harsh voice erupted in strident temper. "Yes, I know I owe you a lot, Mr Bellamy, but not that girl. She's never brought me anything but misery. and despite what you say, I won't stay and work here when she's mistress in this house."

Bellamy's voice uttered some soothing words which Linnet could not make out. Mrs Price grunted.

"Yes, I know, sir. But she could put on that gentle, persuading way of hers before. And then if she didn't get her way—well, you know how her temper blazed, sir, and anyone was her victim. No, I'm not taken in, sir. She's done me enough harm and I was lucky to live to tell the tale. If you leave her, Mr Bellamy, and she's in charge, I'm off, and that's a fact."

Bellamy's voice suddenly startled Linnet, close behind the door at which she crouched. "Have no fear, Mrs Price, I have a plan I am contemplating which could prevent Miss Grey from becoming sole mistress here. Only contemplating the plan at present, you understand, for I am loth to take drastic steps unless it

139

is absolutely necessary. But if I do, there will be no need for you to leave."

"You mean—you'll get rid of her, sir?" Mrs Price's voice was full of hopeful incredulity.

"I shall say no more. Let us say that the sting will be removed from the scorpion's tail. I shall deal with Miss Grey. But promise me you'll stay on at Willerby Manor, Mrs Price?"

"If you can get rid of her, I'll stay."

"I repeat," said Bellamy, low but firmly, "I shall deal with her, but I am hesitant to take steps I may later regret. Now go!"

The doorknob rattled. Linnet turned and fled.

ELEVEN

The nearest way to conceal herself from Bellamy's view was down the staircase, and Linnet fled as swiftly and silently as a bird. Mrs Price was undoubtedly coming downstairs too, to return to the kitchen quarters, so Linnet hastened to the garden-room out of sight.

Rupert Manning was lazing indolently on one of the wicker chairs, but he straightened when Linnet entered, and his handsome face clouded. He stood politely as she came forward, but did not venture to speak. Linnet felt that explanation and apology were due to him after last night, and she smiled pleasantly as she sat down, indicating to him to sit beside her. Rupert stood stiffly, as if undecided what to do.

"Mr Manning, I feel I should explain to you," Linnet began, but he cut her short.

"No need, Miss Grey. Marcus has told me."

It was evident just what Marcus had said, for she noted that Rupert now called her Miss Grey. "But please hear my side of the story," she pleaded. "Please sit and listen for a moment, for I have need to speak to someone."

Rupert sat down diffidently, but he was obviously

ill at ease. Out of politeness he could not refuse a charming request, but he was on his guard, she could see.

"I did not mean to deceive you, Mr Manning, believe me, and in truth I did not," Linnet began.

"But you are Miss Grey, are you not?" Rupert's voice was charged with gentle reproach. "You told me your name was Miss Linnet."

"That is so. My full name is Linnet Grey, but I am not Mr Bellamy's ward. Somehow he has been misled into thinking that I am, but I must find some way to rid him of that delusion."

"Delusion?" Rupert's sandy eyebrows rose steeply. "But he has shown me photographs of you from early childhood—you are undoubtedly his ward!"

"I swear I am not, and I beg you to believe me. I admit the resemblance between us is astonishing, and at times I begin to doubt my own sanity, but truly, Mr Manning, I am Linnet Grey, a teacher in London and an orphan. I wish I could prove it to you."

Rupert rose and bowed stiffly. "I wish I could believe you too, Miss Grey, but if you will excuse me, I am to meet Marcus in his study."

Linnet remembered then that he had told her Marcus Bellamy wanted to discuss a problem—concerning her double, he had said. Was Bellamy about to disclose to Rupert the plan he had devised and which she had just overheard him mention to Mrs Price? She called to Rupert as he opened the door to leave.

"Mr Manning—please—I beg you." Rupert turned at the sound of pleading in her voice. "Please, sir, I entreat your help. If Mr Bellamy should plan to do anything that would be of harm to me, you would not let him, would you? You would befriend me in my helplessness, would you not?"

Rupert was staring at her. "Marcus—harm you? He would not harm a soul, Madam, and it is malicious of you to suggest it. Excuse me."

He withdrew swiftly, and Linnet was left to her own thoughts. She bit her lip, regretting her impulsive words, but what else had she been led to think, hearing Bellamy promise Mrs Price he would take drastic action to deal with her? And then another thought struck her. If Bellamy and Rupert were now closeted in deep discussion in the study, then Bellamy's bedroom would be empty and with luck the secretaire still unlocked. Now would be the perfect opportunity, with Cissie and Mrs Price busy preparing lunch, to creep in and inspect the desk's contents undisturbed. Perhaps it might yield some clue as to what Bellamy might have in his scheming mind.

There was no one about as Linnet crossed the wide vestibule, and she went upstairs and along the corridor to Bellamy's room without seeing or hearing anyone. Casting a final, wary look over her shoulder as she grasped the doorknob and seeing all was clear, she went in.

The secretaire was closed but, to her relief, still unlocked. Neat bundles of letters and documents, writing-paper and envelopes filled the pigeonholes, ink and pens lay ready for use in front of a small central drawer. Linnet pushed the pens aside and pulled the drawer open. Three small leather-bound books lay within. She lifted one out and opened it cu-

145

riously. Each page bore a handwritten date at the head, and closely-written minute handwriting below. It was a diary.

She turned back to the beginning of the book, but it bore no owner's name. She looked again at the dates. The entries covered several months, and the diary ended just two years ago. That was the critical time— the time they claimed she, or the heiress they believed her to be, had run away from this place.

But whose diary was it? Bellamy's? Reading the tiny, closely-written words would probably very soon reveal that, but it was unsafe to stay in this room to read. It would be better to return to the safety of her own room. Having no pocket in which to secrete the diary, Linnet curled her fingers tightly about it so as to conceal it as far as possible in the palm of her hand, replaced the pens in front of the little drawer, and closed the secretaire.

Hearing no sound in the corridor outside, she slipped out and away along the passage to her own room unperceived. There she sat on the edge of the bed and sighed with relief, but as she was uncurling her fingers from the little book she remembered the peephole high in the wall, and glanced up.

That hole must be filled in first before she could read the diary in peace. She pushed the book under the bed coverlet and climbed on the chair again, then looked about for something with which to fill the hole. Then she noticed a corner of yellowing paper protruding from the crack between the top of the high mantelpiece and the cornice. She pulled and tugged until the paper came free. It was a large sheet of paper, soot-stained and smudged, and with writing on it. Linnet peered. Some random phrases in French, like a child's exercise. She tore off the blank lower portion, screwed it up, spat on it and rolled it until it became pliable, then pushed it into the hole.

Having kneaded and pushed until the ball of paper was firmly wedged, Linnet climbed down from her chair, satisfied, and from a lifetime's training of tidiness at Madame Roland's she unthinkingly screwed up the remainder of the dirty sheet of paper and threw it into the empty grate. Then she sat down to read in peace. With luck, no one would disturb her now until the gong rang for lunch.

At first, Linnet found the spidery, minute handwriting extremely difficult to decipher, but gradually she became accustomed to it.

It was too feminine a hand to be Marcus Bellamy's, and as Linnet made out the words it seemed even less likely that these were his sentiments. It began with "My most secret diary, to which I shall commit my innermost thoughts, having no bosom friend in whom I may confide." The words, pathetic as they were, roused little sympathy in Linnet, for she considered the writer to be frankly self-pitying in beginning a diary thus. Unashamedly she read on.

"In this new year, 1880, I fervently hope that life will come at last to Willerby, for life has been miserable and uneventful since Papa's death. Nothing ever happens here. But this year will be different—I will it to be so, and I shall so contrive as to make it be so. No one and nothing shall prevent me."

A headstrong, wilful creature, this, thought Linnet.

It could be the diary of none other than the mysterious Miss Grey, Marcus's ward. Was she unhappy simply because of Papa's death? Linnet read on.

"Everyone and everything seems to conspire against me, to prevent me from enjoying myself. Marcus is hard and cold and apparently believes enjoyment to be sinful, for he never laughs. Nor does he ever become angry. I think I shall try to make him angry with me, for his calm forbearance drives me to distraction."

There, apparently, full of resolve for the New Year, the writer had finished the first day's thoughts for 1880. The second day's account bemoaned the fact that Christmas festivities in Willerby Manor had consisted only of a fine dinner on Christmas Day, but no guests had been invited, while at other houses merrymaking was still no doubt going on until Twelfth Night brought a halt to the festive season.

"What a dull life it is here, to be sure! What a mad family the Greys must have been, to build a house in such a remote, desolate place! I know now why my mother begged Papa to take her away from Willerby and why he was so full of remorse that he did not pay heed to her, for I too loathe the house! Marcus can preach till doomsday that it is my inheritance, but I want no part of it. As soon as I am free I shall leave it, never to return."

The next day's thoughts recorded Miss Grey's hatred, not only of the house but of its gloomy occupants too. Linnet smiled as she read the writer's opinion of the housekeeper. "Mrs Price is a miserable hag! She hates me as heartily as I detest her, the cat. She has

148

never forgotten the prank I played on her as a child, and bears me malice to this day. But how was I to know, a mere child of twelve or so, that a practical joke would cause such mischief? It was innocently intended, but she blames me still for the dreadful consequences, though I am positive it was not my doing."

What prank, Linnet wondered? And what terrible consequence had befallen? Her eye ran on down the page, and the next few words made her catch her breath.

"She guards the West Tower like an evil witch, glowering at me with baleful eye if ever she sees me in the corridor that leads to it. But if she fears that I shall go up there, then she is mistaken, for nothing on earth would induce me to climb those steps! I fear the dreaded thing that walks there too much!"

Linnet turned the page hastily, but the writer's account of the thing in the tower did not go on. Over the page a new day had brought new thoughts to the discontented ward.

"Another dreary, uneventful day! Oh, Lord, I must do something soon to enliven Willerby or I shall go mad! No new faces to see but that miserable, carping Price and my stern guardian, and the ubiquitous, silent Otto! How I loathe that creature! Whatever possessed Marcus to bring that great lumbering ox of a fellow back with him from Central Europe, I shall never know!

"I *must* do something—but what? Set fire to the stables perhaps? But no, my lovely black mare Jester might be harmed, and she is the one creature I would not harm, my glistening black beauty! And so clever and proud! I'd swear she has Arab blood in her ancestry, so mettlesome and fiery she is. And I am glad that she will respond to no one but me. No, I cannot risk harm to her. I must think deeply, and contrive some other way to amuse myself."

Linnet glanced up from the diary at the clock on the mantelshelf. It had crept on relentlessly towards noon, and soon the house would become busy again as the occupants prepared for lunch. She had better return the diary to Bellamy's desk before its absence was noticed.

But she was reluctant to part with the little book which revealed so much about Bellamy's ward. She flicked the pages over to the end and read again.

"My plans are laid. I shall wait until it is time for evening service on Sunday and then I shall feign a headache at the last moment and decline to go to church with Marcus. I have a little bag already packed in the bottom of my wardrobe and I know the time of the London train. With my new month's allowance from Marcus I should have more than sufficient to keep me in a hotel until I find work. Oh! How I look forward to my adventure! Marcus will scarcely believe it that I am gone, for I have given no hint to anyone!

"I shall work and earn a living, and I shall be my own mistress at last, no longer slave to a rambling mansion I hate! Farewell Willerby, farewell Marcus! I leave behind nothing that I love—save Jester, my lovely mare. Instead I shall leave behind all that I hate most strenuously. I salute London and a wonderful, brave, new, free life!"

So that was it. Linnet reflected as she closed the diary and rose to go back to Bellamy's room. That was how the lonely, discontented heiress had contrived to find enjoyment for herself—by running away from a place she hated to a new life in London. Where was she now, and what was she doing? Had London been kind to her, or was she now starving and lonely, longing to make amends and come home?

Linnet's thoughts rambled on in this fashion as she walked slowly to Bellamy's bedroom. Was pride keeping Miss Grey away from Willerby Manor, a defiant girl too proud to admit her mistake and defeat? Or had she found the exuberance she craved in the capital, and discovered contentment at last?

Outside Bellamy's door Linnet stopped, her hand on the doorknob. Would the secretaire still be unlocked, or had Bellamy been back to his room and re-locked it while she was engrossed in the diary? As she was about to turn the knob, low voices came to her ears. Bellamy was inside, talking to someone else! Had he discovered that the diary was gone? If not, perhaps her chance would come to replace it when he and his companion left the room. She decided to wait in the vicinity of his room and take the chance if it arose.

The door suddenly burst open. Linnet retreated hastily round the angle of the corridor corner, her face scalding at the thought that she might have been seen and been accused of eavesdropping. Rupert Manning's voice echoed along the passage towards her.

"You can't be serious, Marcus! Tell me you don't mean it!"

"But I am—in deadly earnest." Bellamy's measured tones were low but full of resolve.

"But you can't stand the girl—you've always said so!"

"True enough. But dire need forces drastic action, my friend, and I can see no other way out of the situation."

Their voices died away on a diminuendo as the two men walked along the corridor away from Linnet and towards the main staircase. Now the room was empty, and Linnet's chance had come. She slipped quietly into the room. The desk was closed, but not locked! She breathed a sigh of relief as she replaced the diary exactly where she had found it and hastened quietly from the room again.

Outside in the corridor she breathed deeply, and then stopped with a gasp. The air was heavy with the smell of violets! Yet a few seconds ago, as she had waited here, there had been no such odour. Someone had been here in the last few moments and had brought the perfume—and had probably seen her entering Marcus Bellamy's room. Who was this silent, unobtrusive person who spied on her every move? And why?

The gong sounded for lunch, cutting short Linnet's perplexed self-questioning. It was only as she descended the stairs to go to the dining-room that she recalled Rupert's bewildering query as he talked with Bellamy. What was it Bellamy had told him he proposed to do with the girl—herself, undoubtedly? By the tone of Rupert's voice it was something terrible and unexpected, but Bellamy's voice had been nothing if not determined. And had he not spoken earlier to Mrs Price of taking "drastic steps" to stop his ward from doing further harm?

Linnet's fears, subdued until now, began to bubble to the surface again. With such a morose, uncommunicative character as Bellamy, who could tell what evil depths might lurk beneath that seemingly calm exterior? And then there was the malevolent, ever-present scent of violets, haunting her every step.

Linnet felt decidedly uneasy as she entered the dining-room and sat down for lunch.

TWELVE

Lunch was a deadly affair. Little conversation was exchanged between the two men, and Linnet said not a word, for she did not know how to address a man who presented a threat to her. Possibly he was even threatening her life!

That was a grim thought that robbed Linnet completely of her appetite. She regarded the two men surreptitiously now and again, and saw that they too were eyeing her thoughtfully in return. What thoughts were passing through their minds, she wondered. If Marcus Bellamy planned to do her harm, was Rupert Manning perhaps now feeling compassionate towards her? He had seemed a man of sensitivity and honest enough—surely he would come over to her aid now if Bellamy were about to attack her in some way.

Conversation revived a little over dessert, and Bellamy looked up towards Linnet with a hint of a smile. "Would you care to visit the stables after lunch, my dear? I have made one or two slight alterations there that might interest you."

Linnet agreed quickly, glad of any opportunity to get out of the claustrophobic atmosphere of the

157

manor for a while. Rupert joined them as they went out of the main door and down the steps.

A long gravel path curled away through the shrubberies and around the corner of the house. A chill wind whipped a few brown desiccated leaves from under the hedge and tossed them playfully about. Linnet was glad she had had the foresight to fetch her warm ulster before venturing out of doors, and welcomed the warmth of Rupert's hand as it slid politely under her elbow. Bellamy strode alongside stiffly, as if unaware of her presence.

At the stable door Otto waited. He grunted, and pushed the doors open for them to enter, pulling his cap off his greasy black hair as he did so. Bellamy nodded and passed inside, and the others followed.

"You will see," Bellamy said as they stood in the warmly foetid air inside, smelling of hay and horses and dung, "that I have renewed some of the timbers of the stalls. Jinty here," he said, turning to indicate a heavy-limbed grey staring at them from over the stall, "had done a pretty good job of kicking the old rotten timber to pieces and it had to be renewed."

Linnet sauntered along the stalls, looking at the sombre-eyed equine occupants. At the last stall she came face to face with a graceful black horse whose nostrils flared suspiciously at her approach. It was a beautiful horse, glossy and black as night, and she backed and whinnied as Linnet stood and watched her. Linnet knew at once whose horse it was.

"Jester," she breathed, half under her breath, but Bellamy heard her. He came to stand close by her.

"So you recognise her? But then, I thought you

158

could not fail to recognise the one being you ever cared for in your life." He smiled sardonically. "And you tried to convince me that you were not my ward. And at times I came near to believing you, cunning creature that you are. But now I know for certain. Have no fear, I have tended your precious Jester well and she is in fine fettle. Will you ride her now?"

Bellamy turned and beckoned Otto to open up the stall and saddle the horse. Otto lumbered forward and Linnet took a step back. She had never ridden a horse in her life and had no conception of how one even mounted.

"I—I—no, no thank you, not today," she stuttered, then cursed herself for not repeating that she was not his ward and could not ride. But already Otto was in with the horse, soothing her with strange, low sounds so that she would stand still to be saddled.

"Go on, now," Bellamy urged. "I know how you must have missed her, and she you. Go for a ride around the grounds—but do not attempt to ride out of the gate, for you will not escape again."

He gave her a helping push forward, and Linnet stumbled inside the stall. The mare's nostrils flared widely, and she backed and threw back her head and made a frightening sound that made Linnet's blood turn cold. Otto looked startled. The mare neighed loudly again, the whites of her eyes gleaming in the half-light, and Linnet turned and hurried out. Bellamy's dark face was creased in a deeply puzzled frown. Rupert was bewildered too, Linnet could see.

"Then let us return to the house if you will not ride, for the weather is turning colder," Bellamy said at last, and turned and strode out of the stables. Rupert followed with Linnet, taking her elbow once more. Outside they could see Bellamy's tall, lean frame already nearing the house steps.

"Strange," Rupert commented as they followed, "but that mare acted as if she distrusted you."

"Because she does not know me," Linnet said quietly.

"Yes, that is how it appeared."

"Because she does not. Now will you believe me, Mr Manning? I am not Mr Bellamy's ward, but Linnet Grey, a total stranger to this place."

"Indeed, I find it hard to believe you are Miss Grey, for often I have heard of how she and Jester were so well-attuned to each other. And Jester would not have forgotten her, I am sure."

Linnet walked on, deep in thought. She glanced up at the ivy-covered house and recognised the window of her bedroom, with the narrow balcony outside. She remembered then the light that appeared from time to time at night, crossing her window, and looked to see where the balcony led.

At one end it led down a narrow stone staircase to the gravel path beneath. Linnet followed it back with her eyes to see where the other end led—and heard her own breath catch in an audible gasp. At the far end of the house, under the West Tower, the balcony came to a halt under another flight of stone steps that led up to the very summit of the tower. So whoever passed her window came from the tower to the garden below.

Rupert led Linnet indoors, then excused himself,

saying he had papers to attend to. Linnet climbed the stairs and returned to her own room, and sat brushing her hair while thoughts whirled in a tumult in her brain. Mrs Price had said that the tower was deserted, unused nowadays; and Cissie—what was it the maidservant had said about an old legend concerning the tower? That the ghost of a faithless wife, walled-up there for her sins, haunted the place, and that it brought doom to those who heard her cries. And Linnet had heard those cries—or, at any event, someone's cries in the gloomy tower. And she had seen the flickering light that Cissie had identified as a will-o'-the-wisp, or corpsecandle as she called it, and that too portended doom.

Linnet shivered and tried to brush the frightening thoughts away. But perhaps Cissie, foolish as she was, had spoken unwitting truth, for did it not now seem that Marcus Bellamy was plotting mischief against her in mistake for his ward?

The afternoon dusk was closing in fast. In the gloom, with not even a fire lit in the hearth to alleviate it, the room had a strangely chill and oppressive air. Linnet wished it was time for dinner so she could go down and join the others.

Then suddenly she paused, the hairbrush half-way to her head. A light footstep outside the door caused a floorboard to creak. Was she being spied upon again? Linnet put down the brush and crept to the door, leaning her cheek against the wood to listen. A gentle sob, escaping on a lightly-drawn breath, came to her ears. Who on earth could be listening at her door in tears? The uneasy thought flitted through her brain again of the weeping ghost, but Linnet banished it quickly. She was walled-up anyway, and could scarcely go wandering about the corridors in the afternoon.

After a moment of indecision, Linnet wrenched the door open. The corridor was empty. Linnet stepped out to see further along. She could not swear to it, but in the half-light she could be forgiven for imagining that she saw the door leading to the tower closing silently. Bustling footsteps in the other direction made her turn. Cissie was coming briskly towards her, her pale face alight with alarm.

"Oh, Miss, there you are. I was getting a bit worried about you," she said, her face visibly registering relief at the sight of Linnet. She wiped her brow jerkily with the hem of her apron.

"Worried about me, Cissie? Why?"

"Cause I keep hearing them talking about you, Miss, and how they would be well rid of you."

"Who says that? Tell me."

"Well, Mrs Price, first of all. She told me she was going to tell the master either you went or she did, 'cause there wasn't room for both of you in the same house."

Linnet felt a measure of relief. That much she already knew from the conversation she had overheard in Bellamy's study. But Cissie had said "first of all"— who else had said it? She asked the maidservant.

"Mr Bellamy it was, to Mr Manning. Mrs Price sent me up to the study with wine for the two gentlemen when they was busy talking in there this morning.

162

They didn't seem to notice me, 'cause they went on talking while I was making up the fire."

"And what did Mr Bellamy say?"

"He told Mr Manning he had a plan to do with you, one he'd already spoken of, and Mr Manning said he didn't like it, and he'd have no part in it."

"Did you gather what the plan was, Cissie?" Linnet took hold of the girl's hands in her eagerness to hear, but Cissie shook her head sadly.

"No, Miss. The master said they'd talk about it again after dinner tonight. I could listen, if you like," she added, a gleam lightening her pale eyes as the thought struck her.

Linnet hesitated to encourage the girl to do something so underhand and reprehensible that it could cost her her job, but dire straits called for stern measures.

"It could be dangerous for you, Cissie. If you are discovered you would be dismissed instantly, with no reference. But I need help. . . ." Linnet's eyes searched the other girl's, and the maid smiled.

"I'll be very quiet, Miss. They'll never know I'm there."

"And Mrs Price?"

"She's never about in the evenings. I don't know where she goes—to her own room, perhaps, but she's never around, so she won't see me."

"But when do you go home, down to the village?"

"Not till nine tonight. Tell yer what, Miss, if I hear anything I think yer ought to know, I could meet yer before I leave and tell you."

163

"Yes, thank you, Cissie. Where would be the best place for us to meet?"

Cissie thought for a moment. "Well, the gentlemen might be still in the library, but the music-room will be empty. I'll see you there at nine."

Linnet nodded in agreement. The maid, apparently very pleased at having a mission of such importance to carry out, hurried off downstairs again and Linnet returned to her room until the gong boomed for dinner. But it was a solitary repast, for neither Bellamy nor Rupert Manning appeared.

Mrs Price served Linnet in silence, and Linnet could feel the woman's baleful stare piercing her back. Was it true, as the diarist had recorded, that the housekeeper and Bellamy's ward had a mutual hatred of each other? And why? What was the malicious prank that had caused Mrs Price such dreadful consequences?

Linnet made a sudden resolve. For the moment she would play the part of bellamy's ward and tackle Mrs Price.

"Mrs Price, may I ask you something?"

The housekeeper stared back, her small dark eyes full of suspicion. "What is it, Miss Grey?"

"Why do you dislike me so? What is it I did to you that was so dreadful you can never forgive me?"

The woman's eyes grew wider. "You—can ask me that? Can you have forgotten?"

"Maybe I was too young to recall. Refresh my memory, Mrs Price, and tell me what I did."

"You wasn't too young to remember. You was

twelve years old and far too grown up for such tricks. Even a twelve-year-old knows that tripping someone on the stairs is dangerous."

"I? Did that?" Linnet was incredulous.

"You know you did. A wire stretched across the top step can't be seen in the half-light, and well you knew it, you mischievous child. And you never changed. Setting fire to the hay-ricks, cutting down all the master's flowers soon as they bloomed—you never stopped doing all the damage your cunning mind could think up. And you ask me why I dislike you. Dislike! There's a genteel name for what I feel for you!"

Linnet was staring open-mouthed at the new picture which was emerging of the other Miss Grey. But had the fall on the stairs injured the housekeeper? She walked with no hint of a limp or any other disability. Surely if she had escaped with only minor hurts she would not have brooded over the incident and borne malice for so long?

"The fall on the stairs—were you hurt, Mrs Price? I truly do not remember."

The housekeeper banged a tray down on the table. "Indeed you have a mighty convenient memory, or lack of it. Do you not recall the night of pain I spent, and how you shrieked and wailed when the morning came and you saw what the night's events brought forth? You screamed with terror, and vowed you wished never to see it again. Can you not remember why you hate the tower so, and the creature that lurks there, forbidden to come out?"

165

She snatched up the tray and marched quickly out of the room, leaving Linnet bewildered and afraid. What thing in the tower? And what connection could it have with Mrs Price's fall so long ago?

All evening Linnet's thoughts raced on in a jumble of fears and doubts that led her nowhere. Only two solutions seemed practicable—to devise some means to escape from this house of mystery and menace, or to stay and bluster it out, in an attempt to uncover the mystery. But which was she to do? And how was she to escape if that seemed the wiser course?

A letter to Madame Roland; that was it. A letter explaining she had been kidnapped and asking her to inform the police of her whereabouts. That would bring the police down here in a hurry, and Bellamy and his ward could work out their own salvation. But the problem remained: how to get a letter to the post. Perhaps Cissie would help.

Cissie. That reminded Linnet of their assignation. The clock was nearing nine. Perhaps she should go down to the music-room now, for it would appear less suspicious if she were to arrive early and be playing the piano if someone should intrude. Linnet went downstairs.

In the music-room a fire glowed in the hearth, though no lamps were lit. Linnet sat in a deep arm-chair and waited in the firelight. The clock on the mantelshelf struck nine, but no Cissie appeared. The minutes ticked inexorably on, but by half past nine she still had not come.

Linnet rose wearily from her chair. Obviously, the girl was not going to appear now. She opened the door and went out into the corridor and found Rupert pacing agitatedly towards her.

"Miss Grey! I've been looking for you. Marcus wants to see you in his study."

time and went out into the corridor and found Kim
constantly speaking, her voice low
After a while I said, looking up you. I mean
where do we go from here?

THIRTEEN

With some degree of agitation Linnet made her way to the study. Was Marcus Bellamy about to reveal to her what course of action he had decided upon with regard to her, or was he going to keep his plan a secret and somehow trap her unawares?

She was hardly in a state to think clearly any longer, what with all the revelations she had made today from Mrs Price and the diary, from Cissie and from overheard conversations. This whole episode of her life was so confused and meaningless that it had the wavery, unreal and frightening quality of a nightmare from which she devoutly hoped she would soon awaken.

Marcus Bellamy was sitting behind his desk, leaning back with one leg casually crossed over the other, and drawing languidly on his pipe. He did not appear tense and poised, like a man about to commit murder, but how could she tell, for she did not know this man and how coolly he might approach such an action.

He appeared deep in thought, his hard, clear-cut profile starkly silhouetted against the oil lamp on the table behind him. It was a handsome face, thought Linnet, if it were not for the cold severity in the eyes.

He turned then, as if he had just become aware of her presence. "Please sit, my dear, for there is a matter I wish to discuss with you."

Linnet sat nervously on the edge of the chair before his desk and waited. Bellamy stood watching her and puffing on his pipe abstractedly. The clock ticked loudly in the silence of the study, and Linnet began to feel a prickle of irritation. What was there about this man's commanding presence that kept her pinioned there, like an errant schoolchild awaiting punishment? His manner was one that demanded instant compliance, and Linnet was angry with herself for submitting meekly to his arrogance. After all, she was not his ward, nor was any special deference due to him although he was a gentleman and she but a poor teacher. He was still making no attempt to speak. Linnet decided to launch in on the offensive.

"You wished to speak to me, I believe? If not, I shall leave you."

The thoughtful dark eyes came to life at once. "No, do not go. I was hesitating how to broach the matter to you."

"The best method is always the most direct, I find," Linnet retorted sharply.

There was a glimmer of amusement in the eyes. "Very well, let it be so. Tell me, my dear, do you dislike me any less than you did?"

Linnet was taken aback at his question. She hedged. "I like you neither more nor less than I ever did," she said at length.

"You do not find me totally repulsive then?" The eyes manoeuvred and seemed to pierce her very soul.

172

"Repulsive? That is a strong word, Mr Bellamy. No, I do not find you repulsive. Overbearing and dictatorial, perhaps, but not repulsive."

"But, on the other hand, not a congenial companion, I take it?"

"No."

"I see."

The penetrating gaze was diverted then to the papers on his desk, and Bellamy's high forehead furrowed into a frown. There was another long silence.

"Well?" Linnet demanded at last. She was not going to allow him to regain control of the situation again.

Marcus looked up and took a deep breath before he began. "I have deliberated long over what I am now going to propose to you, and discussed it at length with Rupert, who is not at all in favour of my plan. But I can see no other remedy. But first let me ask you again—are you willing to take over Willerby and run the estate when it becomes yours?"

"I am not." Linnet chose her words with care. How else could she answer when the estate was not hers to claim, and her questioner refused to believe who she was?

"Then there is no alternative. I must do what is to be done."

At last, thought Linnet, he is going to tell me! But at the precise moment when she leaned forward so as to miss none of his next words, a crash echoed along the corridor outside and a piercing scream rent the air.

Bellamy looked up, startled, and was at the door before Linnet's gasp had died away.

"No, you stay here—I shall deal with it," Bellamy said abruptly as she made to follow him, and, thrusting her back, he went out and slammed the door. Linnet hovered just inside, uncertain whether to follow him or obey. Running footsteps passed the door and agitated voices murmured in the distance, rising and falling like waves on the shore, but Linnet could make out nothing.

That scream was hideous. Linnet could hear it again in memory, and put her fingers to her ears. She trembled involuntarily and Cissie's words came back to her about the walled-up ghost and its cries in the night. Oh, if only she could get away from the strange happenings and atmosphere laden with foreboding that overshadowed this house!

The voices and footsteps died away. In a moment the door opened and Bellamy entered, closely followed by a bewildered Rupert, whose dressing-gown, awkwardly buttoned over his nightshirt, revealed that he was preparing for bed when the noise disturbed him.

"Are you all right, Miss Grey?" he asked, as he pattered in in flapping slippers, then his tense look relaxed as he saw that all was well with her.

"Miss Grey is perfectly well, Rupert. Now go back to bed, there's a good chap. There's nothing to concern yourself over," Marcus assured him.

"But the crash—and the scream," Rupert persisted.

"A slight mishap, but, as you see, my ward is quite

174

well and unharmed, so please return to bed. We shall talk in the morning."

"Very well." Rupert's voice betrayed his reluctance to leave the mystery unsolved, but he too, Linnet noted, always deferred to Bellamy's stronger persuasion. He shuffled amiably enough back to bed.

Bellamy faced Linnet. "And you too, my dear, I think it time you were in bed also."

"But we were talking! You were about to tell me of a plan," Linnet protested.

"I was. But the moment has gone. Tomorrow possibly we will reopen the subject. But for now, good night, my dear, and sleep well."

His turned back indicated that he had finished with her for tonight. Disappointment filled Linnet as she went, and was quickly replaced with anger at herself. Why did she accept dismissal so meekly? Why had she not demanded to know what he was about to say? But it was too late now. Bellamy's door was closed.

She walked disconsolately away, then stopped. Damn the man! Why should she subject herself to his whims? If he truly believed her to be his ward, then he owed her a measure of respect! She would go back to him now, this minute, and demand to know what he planned to do with her!

She rapped defiantly on Bellamy's door and waited. When no answer came, she rapped again, more loudly this time. After a moment Bellamy's head appeared.

"Well? What is it?"

"Mr Bellamy, I demand to know what you are planning to do. It is my right to know."

175

"In the morning I shall tell you—if I have not had second thoughts on the matter."

"The morning will not do. I desire to know now, tonight."

Bellamy opened the door a little wider and smiled. "Now, it seems, you are reverting to something more like your true self," he commented drily. "I wondered how long you could maintain the meek and decorous attitude you have had of late. But as you well know, my pet, I am not an impulsive man, nor am I to be rushed. I shall speak when I am ready."

Linnet's cheeks flushed at being called his pet. "That will not do!" she cried impulsively, "nor am I your pet! My name is Linnet."

"So you told me. A pretty name, and no doubt you chose it because you felt it suited your feeling of being a little bird trapped in a cage it hated. So be it. I shall call you Linnet—but I will not be coerced into speaking to you until I am ready. Good night."

He closed the door firmly. Linnet felt hot tears of frustration and anger welling in her eyes, and rushed blindly back to her own room. How could he treat her so, with an air of paternal indulgence, like a father watching a spoilt child displaying its tantrums! She did not want him to humour her thus!

She lay awake half the night, tossing and dozing fitfully in snatches of sleep that were riddled with hideous dreams. Then suddenly she stiffened. She was awake now, and whispered voices floated in the air. Someone was out in the corridor.

As she lay and listened, the whispers ceased and

silence pervaded the house again. Linnet rose, flung a dressing-gown about her shoulders and went to the door. Still silence. She opened the door and went out.

Not a sound nor a shadow disturbed the dark silence outside. But she knew she had not imagined the whispers—*someone* had been here, but a moment ago. She crept towards the passage end, and stopped by the door leading to the tower staircase. When her eyes became accustomed to the gloom she saw that the door stood ajar. Linnet pushed it open.

A shaft of moonlight from a high, narrow window-slit on the stairs illuminated the lower part of the steps, gleaming whitely under the light. And on the third step lay a small black object. Linnet approached it curiously. As her fingers reached out to pick it up they encountered a sticky substance on the step beside it, but Linnet ignored it as she looked closely at what she had found.

It was a shoe. A left shoe, made of cloth, of the kind that servants wore. Of course, it was Cissie's, she recognised it now! But if her shoe was here, then where was Cissie? What had she been doing in the region of the West Tower that she dreaded so?

If she had not come here voluntarily, then had someone brought her here against her will? That would at least account for that awesome scream and for why she had not kept her rendezvous with Linnet in the music-room tonight. But where was she now?

Then the strange, sickly-sweet smell drifted to Linnet's nostrils again, the scent of violets she had come to associate with menace. Linnet, scenting danger, fled precipitately back to the sanctuary of her room, still clutching the shoe in her hand and her heart pounding with trepidation.

There she lit a candle with shaking fingers and caught sight of a stain on her fingertips. She bent close to the candle to examine it. Of course, the sticky substance on the stairs. But what was it, brown and glutinous and unpleasant?

Blood! It was blood! Linnet recoiled in horror, rubbing her hands involuntarily across her dressing-gown to get rid of the vile stuff. Then the realisation came to her that if blood lay next to Cissie's shoe, then Cissie must have been hurt.

Or killed even? Linnet shuddered. No, surely not. Not even Marcus Bellamy with his cold, scheming manner could do such a thing, even if he had guessed that Cissie was in league with Linnet.

And in any event, Bellamy had been with Linnet in his study when that horrible scream had ripped into their conversation, cutting it short at a point when Bellamy had been about to clear some of the mystery that enshrouded this house. So he, at any rate, could not have harmed Cissie.

Linnet paced her room in an agony of indecision. Should she go immediately, long past midnight though it was, and show Bellamy the shoe and demand an explanation, or should she wait until morning? But by then it might be too late. Who knew whether Cissie was dead or lying injured and untended somewhere?

At last Linnet lay down and fell asleep, to be awakened in the morning by Mrs Price. Linnet looked at

178

the housekeeper closely, but the woman's hooded eyes revealed nothing. Linnet decided to find out from her what she knew.

"Mrs Price, tell me—did you hear the commotion last night?"

Mrs Price fixed her with a sphinx-like, inscrutable stare. "What commotion?"

"A crash and a scream—and people hurrying to and fro. What was it?"

"I don't know."

"And where is Cissie this morning? Why hasn't she brought me my tea?"

"She isn't here today."

"Why not?"

"She can't. She's had a slight accident and will be staying at home for a few days."

"I see." Linnet's gaze wandered to the dressing-table, to where she had left the tell-tale shoe last night. It was not there. Someone must have taken it while she slept! She opened her mouth and was about to remonstrate with the housekeeper, and then thought better of it. The woman would undoubtedly deny all knowledge of it, so what was the use?

No, it was Marcus Bellamy she must tackle. He was the man behind all the strange events in this house, she was sure of it. She must beard him and remain unmoved by any excuses, worrying him steadfastly until the truth was out. And today, this very morning.

Mrs Price having gone, Linnet rose and dressed. If Bellamy did not appear at breakfast, then she would march resolutely to his study straight afterwards. Or, better still, find Rupert first and take him with her, for now it was apparent that his sympathies were leaning in her direction.

A bundle of sticks in the hearth caught Linnet's eye as she finished dressing. Mrs Price was apparently going to light a fire here today, and would no doubt soon reappear with a bucket of coal. Linnet caught sight of a solitary piece of paper in the empty grate. Ah yes, the yellowing sheet of paper with the Willerby heiress's French exercises scribbled upon it. On an impulse Linnet stooped down and retrieved it, smoothing out the crumpled sheet until the spidery words became visible.

There were several sentences, evidently translated from English into French for the benefit of some unknown tutor, and then a piece of what appeared to be verse. Linnet carried it to the window to see better.

"*Petit oiseau captif*," it began. Linnet smiled, recalling how Marcus Bellamy had compared her to a captive bird in a cage.

> "*Petit oiseau captif*
> *Dans une cage dorée*
> *Voudrait s'envoler*
> *Personne ne le permets.*"

A sad little poem. Little bird, caged in a gilded trap, would like to fly away, but no one will let him. The young heiress evidently found no consolation in the thought of future riches if she longed so much to flee from Willerby Manor.

But then Linnet saw that lower down the page, half-obliterated by soot and grime, lay another line,

180

evidently an afterthought to the poem. She screwed up her eyes to read it.

"*Prisonnière, Chantal ne chant plus.*" A prisoner, Chantal sings no more. Chantal! The word sprang from the page and hit Linnet so hard she gasped. Chantal! A French name, like the actress Chantal Legris. Chantal Legris . . . and "Legris" was the French for "grey"! Of course, Chantal Grey! Chantal Legris was the hated heiress of Willerby!

FOURTEEN

Many things began to fit into place now for Linnet, although she was still stunned by her discovery. Chantal Legris, the beautiful actress fêted and toasted by all London society, was the girl who had been entrusted to Marcus Bellamy's care, and who hated the isolation of Willerby so intensely that she had run away to London two years ago.

Linnet recalled the minute handwriting in the girl's diary, of how she hoped to find work in the city. Apparently she had, and, what was more, had eventually made a great success of it. Bellamy had said he had been unable to trace her—until that night at the theatre. So it was Chantal's rise to fame which had led Bellamy to her, to try to bring her back to face her responsibilities, but instead he had found Linnet.

She smiled ruefully at the recollection of the way he had accosted her—"Will you come home with me?"—and how she had mistaken his intention. By now she knew better than to believe Marcus Bellamy capable of accosting a woman for his own pleasure, for he was far too stern and cold. He had obviously mistaken her for Chantal. In the half-light of the gas lamp outside the theatre his mistake was perhaps understandable. And then Linnet recalled the sensation she had experienced in the theatre—the feeling of familiarity about Chantal, down there on the stage below. Now she understood—it was the actress's resemblance to herself, the feeling of looking into a mirror and seeing her own reflection that had only vaguely obtruded itself on to her consciousness. It was this resemblance which had fooled Marcus Bellamy.

But still, it was an odd coincidence that both she and her double shared the same surname. Now, at any rate, she understood the misapprehension under which Bellamy—and Mrs Price too—had been labouring. Now she could go to him and explain.

Mrs Price reappeared at that point, staggering with the weight of the bucket of coal she carried and muttering about the stairs and having much to do. Linnet left her to see to the fire and went downstairs.

Bellamy was just finishing breakfast in the dining-room. There was no sign of Rupert Manning. Linnet hastened towards Bellamy eagerly, holding out the piece of yellowed paper.

"Look what I found, Mr Bellamy, behind the mantelpiece! It suddenly makes all clear to me—your ward is Chantal, and you mistook me for her. But it is Chantal you are seeking—Chantal Legris—and she is still in London!"

Bellamy wiped his mouth leisurely on his napkin and pushed his chair back, ignoring the paper she held out to him. "Now listen to me, my little bird," he said, but there was no affection in the words, only a tone of the utmost weariness. "I have endured your game of make-believe long enough. Do you truly ex-

186

pect me to believe that a piece of your own scribbling is going to convince me that you are not Chantal? No, do not interrupt me. I have the evidence of my own eyes. Mrs Price recognises and remembers you well—and did you not give the game away yesterday when you could not resist breathing Jester's name at the sight of her?"

"But you saw how the horse reacted! She did not know me!"

"Did not recognise you instantly, perhaps, after two years. Or was suspicious at your sudden reappearance, for she is a highly-intelligent and highly-bred mare. But whatever the reason, I remain unmoved by your shamming, young lady. You will not evade your duty, and I shall see to it that you do not."

Linnet turned away angrily. What was the use of arguing with such a stubborn, implacable man?

Bellamy rose and made for the door. His hand on the knob, he paused. "I do not know whether you may wish to join us, my dear, but Rupert and I are going to morning service at ten. I know you were not in the habit of church-going in the past, but if you wish to come, you may do so. Rupert is returning to town after lunch."

And he was gone. Linnet fumed at his patriarchal manner, simply informing her that Rupert was leaving and that she could go to church with them if she wished, but no comment that they would welcome her company; no such politeness from him!

Well, if he would not listen to her, then she would go, if only just to vex him with her company which he apparently found so distasteful. If he insisted on treating her as Chantal, then she would jolly well act as Chantal, provoking and annoying him. He would soon learn to regret having abducted her.

Over breakfast Linnet decided to write a brief letter to Madame. It was just possible she might find the opportunity to post it on this, her first excursion out of the manor. The pen in the desk in her—or rather Chantal's—bedroom was reluctant to write after two years' disuse, and scratched and spluttered rebelliously, but Linnet managed to pen a tolerably legible letter. could not resist a smile at the thought of Madame, whose smooth waters were never troubled by drama, learning that one of her junior staff had been kidnapped in mistake for the eminent Mademoiselle Legris. Then, borrowing a fur muff from Chantal's wardrobe, she secreted the letter inside and went down to the vestibule.

She was early, and had to await Bellamy and Rupert for some minutes. Again the strange shiver of familiarity rippled over her in the deserted hallway. It was odd how often she had felt this tremor of half-recognition.

Then the flickeringly-fancied sensation was sent scudding away by the arrival of Rupert Manning. In his dark-grey overcoat he looked broader than usual, its cape giving his thin shoulders the illusion of breadth and strength. He nodded politely, but seemed diffident about speaking to her. Surely he believed her now, however, after witnessing Jester's reaction to her yesterday? Linnet asked him.

"You do believe me now, do you not, Mr Manning? You do believe that I am who I say I am, and not Mr Bellamy's ward?"

Rupert shifted his gaze uncomfortably. "Miss Grey, it matters little what I believe. Marcus is my friend of long standing and I have always trusted him implicitly."

"But now you know he is wrong! You have seen the evidence! I think, in fact, Mr Bellamy is no liar but is guilty only of self-deception; he genuinely believes I am his ward, and I cannot convince him otherwise. But you know, don't you, Mr Manning? You know I speak the truth. Will you not help me? You do not seem a man who would abandon a lady in distress."

Rupert shuffled from foot to foot uneasily while she spoke. He cleared his throat and coughed before replying. "I am sorry. As I said, Marcus is my friend, Miss Grey, and whatever I suspect I cannot betray a friend's trust. I have never had reason to doubt his word—nor have I now, apart from the odd behaviour of the horse. You would not have me betray a long-standing friendship, would you?"

His blue eyes looked at her pleadingly. Linnet turned away in disgust. What a weakling he was, to ignore a woman's pleas and hide behind a façade of pretended loyalty to his friend! He had not a fraction of Bellamy's strength and determination. Linnet was amused. How strange—she was comparing him unfavourably with a man she disliked so much. Bellamy would be amused if he knew she was thinking of him so flatteringly.

189

Bellamy hastened to join them. "I am sorry to have kept you waiting. Is the carriage at the door?"

Linnet watched him as he opened the door and called to Otto. He was a handsome man, there was no doubt of it, and in his overcoat and hat and with a silver-headed cane in his hand he was a most impressive figure of a man. Under other circumstances she might have liked him well, this tall, commanding figure with an air of poise and maturity. Under other circumstances . . . but then, it was useless to daydream. Linnet followed the gentlemen out to the carriage.

Rupert stood by while Bellamy held out his hand to her to help her mount the carriage steps. Was it Linnet's imagination or was there a slight, momentary pressure on her fingers as theirs hands touched? There was certainly a hint of a smile at the corners of those tight lips as she looked back at him askance.

The short journey to the village church was completed in silence, Rupert sinking back into the corner and gazing at the mist-covered countryside outside. Bellamy appeared deep in his own thoughts and never once looked at her. Linnet clutched tightly at the letter hidden in her muff and prayed the chance would come for her to post it.

At a small country church the carriage stopped, and Bellamy helped her alight, but this time she noticed nothing unusual as their hands met. Inside the church Bellamy led the way to a high-backed pew near the front.

The congregation was small, mostly of local farmers and tenants and their families, Linnet guessed by their dress. Their footsteps were quiet as they took their places, but Linnet saw the glances that came her way, and the subdued movements as the heads turned again to murmur to a neighbour, and then more glances. No doubt they too believed that the long-lost heiress had returned to take up her inheritance. Faint whispers echoed across the little stone church, rippling the atmosphere no more than a summer breeze over a field of corn. And in every glance that came her way, Linnet sensed hostility.

Bellamy stopped and waited for her to enter the pew first. Set into a brass plate on the wood was a little white card, "The Grey Family", it read. How many generations of the Greys had worshipped in this church, Linnet wondered idly as she took her seat. It must be wonderful to have a family heritage such as this. If she were Chantal Grey, she would not lightly discard such a heritage.

The service began, and Linnet ceased her speculation. It was a long service, drawn out to interminable length by the vicar's tedious, droning sermon. Linnet felt her head begin to spin. She never could bear enclosed, confined spaces with many bodies for long. She reached into her reticule for her smelling salts, but they were not there. Without them she knew she would faint before long.

She looked at Bellamy in the hope of catching his attention, but he was regarding the vicar, his face furrowed in earnest concentration as the vicar's voice droned on. It was no use, she would have to interrupt him.

"Mr Bellamy, I fear I must go out for a few minutes—the lack of air, you know."

Bellamy rose at once. "I shall come with you," he said.

"No, there is no need. I shall recover as soon as I reach fresh air; do not worry."

Linnet pressed past him and Rupert and walked as quietly as she could up the aisle, hoping her tottering knees would not give way before she reached the door. Outside, she gulped the cold, clammy air gratefully, and felt the encroaching mist in her head begin to dissipate.

The stone wall of the church was cold against her back, even through her ulster. Linnet straightened, deciding to stroll a few yards to ensure she was completely recovered before returning. But as she walked, she became conscious of the paper under her fingers inside the muff. The letter to Madame! She looked about her. There was no sign of Otto and the carriage. No doubt he knew the length of the vicar's sermons and had gone back to the manor until it was time for him to collect the master. If ever there was an opportunity to sneak away undetected, this was it! Neither Bellamy nor Rupert had emerged from the church in search of her.

Linnet looked around. Away across the misty fields she could see a cluster of houses. That was no doubt Willerby village. If she could reach there, perhaps some villager, encouraged by her last sixpence, would take charge of the letter and promise to post it for her.

She glanced back. The church door was still firmly

closed and no one in sight. She crossed the lane and climbed with some difficulty, hampered by her skirts, over the stile and set off across the field. It was not far to the village—half a mile at the most.

The grass was very wet. It soon seeped through the cloth uppers of her boots and made her feet very cold and damp. But as Linnet hastened on, anxious to reach the village before Bellamy discovered the reason for her long absence, the ground became more and more squelchy under her feet. Too late now, however, to think better of it and go back.

But feverishly as she ran, she could make little speedy progress for the soggy ground became suddenly ankle deep in mud, clutching avariciously at her feet and refusing to allow her to run. Linnet stumbled occasionally, unable to keep her balance in the quagmire, and at last she fell forward, taking the brunt of her weight on her hands. Her left arm disappeared under the surface up to beyond her elbow. Linnet stood up slowly, staring at the mud on her arm in disbelief. In that spot the mud must have been well over a foot deep, if not more.

Footsteps squelched close behind her. Linnet turned to see Bellamy closing on her, his face white and rigid with anger.

"You fool! You stupid little fool!" he muttered when at last he reached her. "I thought you knew better than to risk these treacherous marshes alone and unguided! Better people than you have been misled and lost their lives here. How could you be so foolish? You must hate me and Willerby to risk so much to escape!"

Linnet could only stand and stare at him. Of course, she had forgotten she had been warned of the danger of the marshes.

"Well?" Bellamy demanded. "Have you lost your tongue, Miss? What were you planning to do, may I ask? Run away back to London? Have you a confederate waiting with a carriage, perhaps? I cannot think how you managed to plot with a conspirator, for I have had your every movement watched. Did you elude my guard somehow? Out with it! I am your guardian still, remember, and as such I am still responsible for you. What were you going to do?"

Linnet looked down miserably at her muff, its fur now barely recognisable through its thick covering of greasy brown mud. The letter still lay inside.

"I was only going to post a letter," she said miserably, sickened with dismay and frustration at her failure, and feeling an absolute fool to have to stand before him coated in filth like a street urchin.

Bellamy's eyes were glittering at her in silent fury. He looked her slowly up and down.

"Come, let's go home," he said at length, taking her arm firmly and as if unaware of the mud that transferred itself from her to him. "Let's get you out of sight before the congregation comes out and sees you in this disgusting state." His voice expressed the disgust he himself felt for her. He evidently did not believe she was running thus wildly only to post a letter. He still thought her a liar, Linnet thought miserably— oh, how she hated this man!

She submitted meekly to him as he propelled her firmly back in the direction of the church, and helped

194

her clamber ungracefully over the stile. Otto was sitting waiting on the carriage. Bellamy called to him.

"You will drive me and Miss Grey home, and then return for Mr Manning when the service is ended," he told the man, and opened the carriage door for Linnet.

It was a miserable ride. Although Linnet could not bring herself to look Bellamy directly in the face, she knew he was glaring at her with scorn and revulsion as the carriage clattered homeward. Linnet had never felt so humiliated and unhappy in her life. At length she ventured to look up at him shyly. Her lips were curled in derision.

"Do—do you dislike me so much?" she whispered tremulously at last. "Do you find me so distasteful?"

Bellamy's eyes went cold. "Distasteful? Not distasteful, Miss Grey. I find you disgusting."

And he was not referring to her appearance only, Linnet knew. He meant her whole personality repelled him. She wished she could shrivel up and die.

The carriage turned into the gates of Willerby Manor and began the long climb up the tree-lined drive. From under tear-laden eyelashes, Linnet looked up at him and scarcely dared to speak, so full of shame she felt. But she had to know.

"Mr. Bellamy—please tell me—what do you plan to do with me?" After so many hints of the plans he threatened, she must discover what worse could still befall her.

"Plan?" he repeated coolly. "Ah, yes, you refer to our interrupted conversation last night. Well, now I have finally decided. There is no alternative and,

195

much against my own inclination, I have made up my mind to embark upon a project which is distasteful in the extreme to me."

"And that is?"

Bellamy fixed her with his coldly piercing look.

"I shall marry you, Miss Grey."

FIFTEEN

Linnet was so stunned by Bellamy's words that she was rendered speechless, and she could scarcely remember dismounting from the carriage and re-entering Willerby Manor. Through a haze she vaguely heard Bellamy order Mrs Price to see to filling a bath for Miss Grey and laying out fresh clothes for her, and then she followed the housekeeper's shuffling figure upstairs.

Still Bellamy's words kept ringing in her ears: "I shall marry you, Miss Grey!" It was a statement of fact, of determination, not a proposal. He had told her, not asked her if she would marry him. And anyone less like a suitor she could not imagine. His expression had been ice-cold as he spoke the words, and his voice as emotionless as if he had been merely commenting upon the state of the weather. If it had not been so startling it would have been downright amusing, she thought. No pleading suitor on bended knee, this Marcus Bellamy, but a man of iron who would not be thwarted.

But why? That was the puzzling question. Why should Bellamy want to marry her—or his ward, for that matter, if he still believed her so—when he had said he loathed her? He had seemed only too anxious to be quit of his responsibility for her not so long ago.

It was only as Linnet peeled off her mudsoaked clothes and stepped into the steaming water of the bath that she realised how freezingly cold and wet she was. The warm water lapped soothingly about her, and she lay back and luxuriated in the sensation. Gradually the cold numbness faded, and as her circulation returned to normal, so did her brain begin to function once again more clearly.

Of course, she would have to tell Bellamy that his proposal was impossible. Not only was she not Chantal, his ward, but she was also still a minor in law. Nor did she have the slightest inclination to marry him. Not that he was concerned about that, but once he knew and admitted who she really was, he would probably not want to marry her any more than she did him. Imagine it, being wife to an intractable, impossible creature like him! It was unthinkable!

There was nothing else for it. After she had emerged from the bath and dressed in clean, warm clothes which Mrs Price had laid out by the fire, Linnet made resolutely for the study. In her hand she carried the letter she had written so furtively to Madame.

She entered without knocking, her head high and her chin jutted defiantly. Marcus Bellamy looked up from the papers in his hand and took his pipe from his mouth, his eyebrows arched in surprise at her unwarranted intrusion into his sanctum.

"Mr Bellamy, marriage between us is out of the question," Linnet said firmly. "In the first place I am not your ward, and in the second place I am eighteen years of age."

"So you have persisted in maintaining."

"And, in any event, I do not like you."

"Nor I you, my dear, but we cannot have all we would wish for."

"You cannot force me to marry you against my will."

Bellamy smiled. "You have someone else in mind, perhaps?"

Linnet's mouth dropped open. "No, of course not. But I would not take you in default of a better husband."

"Perhaps not. But you have made it clear that you do not wish to manage the estate yourself, and you will need someone to do it in your place. Especially if you are determined to return to London."

"A husband is not necessary for that, Mr Bellamy. Your ward could employ an agent or a lawyer. Could you not act as her lawyer?"

"I was your father's lawyer, not yours. And it is for his sake that I offer marriage."

Linnet's eyes rounded in surprise. "You mean—out of respect for Thomas Grey you would contract yourself in marriage to his daughter—whom you admittedly detest? Why should you be willing to make such a sacrifice?"

Bellamy put down his papers and regarded her earnestly. "Because I loved Thomas like a father, and on his deathbed he asked me whether I would marry you when you came of age if you did not seem capable of managing alone."

"But there is no legal compulsion for you to do this!"

"None. I contracted to be your guardian and care for the estate till your coming of age only. But Thomas suspected that you would perhaps be fickle and feckless like your mother, and he feared that you might fritter away your money and let the estate fall to ruin. So he asked me to keep an eye to you, and never to abandon you to your own weakness. Even, he said, to marry you if I would, so as to keep a rein on your extravagance."

He contemplated the stem of his pipe for a moment before continuing. "Unfortunately, matters turned out very similarly to what he feared. You are feckless and foolish, and I have spent too many years in protecting your interests here at Willerby Manor to be willing to let you undo all my work now. Therefore I propose to marry you and remain here as master, and thus continue to see that Willerby flourishes."

"I see," Linnet murmured. "That would be all very well, Mr Bellamy, if I were your ward, and your ward agreed to your plan. But if you wish to carry it out, then you must go to the Alhambra Theatre in London in search of her, for I am not she."

Bellamy sighed. "Please, Chantal! I beg you to give up this ridiculous farce. If you are only playing for time, it is of no avail."

"But I am not Chantal! See—here is the letter I was running through the marsh to post. Open it—read it! See then if you believe me!"

Bellamy made no move to take the letter Linnet held out to him. She pushed it closer to him. "See the address—to Madame Roland. Here, I will open it for you." She tore it open and handed him the single sheet of paper. Bellamy took it and read it slowly, then looked up at her.

"Now do you believe me? Would I write to a woman and tell her I had been kidnapped in mistake for another if I were truly Chantal?" Linnet demanded angrily. "You are a very hard man to convince, Mr Bellamy, but I hope you believe it now."

Bellamy put the paper down on his desk. "Why should I believe it?" he said evenly. "It is not beyond your devious mind to fake such a letter to try to deceive me. After all, you have not posted it."

"I would have done so if you had not prevented me," Linnet cried. Oh, what a stubborn creature he was! Then suddenly another idea came to her. She sat on the chair facing him and closed her eyes tightly.

"Tell me, Mr Bellamy, do you know what colour are Chantal's eyes?"

"Of course."

"What are they?"

"Blue."

"Are you positive?"

There was no answer. Linnet was tempted to open her eyes to see his reaction, but kept them firmly closed. She was not going to give him a chance to see the colour of her eyes. "Well?" she prompted.

"Yes, I am sure of it. They are blue."

Linnet opened her eyes now with a smile of triumph.

"And what colour are mine, Mr Bellamy?"

Marcus Bellamy put down his pipe and leaned forward across the desk to peer, until his nose was barely an inch from her own. It was an effort for her to stare back unblinkingly. Finally, Bellamy sat back.

"Well? What colour are my eyes?"

"Grey." His voice was low, but the disappointment was evident.

"There now!" Linnet could not resist the tone of triumph. "Will you believe me now?"

Bellamy shrugged and picked up his pipe again. "Grey—blue—there is little difference. It is easy to confuse the two, and in certain lights eyes change colour anyway. No, my dear, I'm afraid your little experiment does not convince me, not in the least. You are wasting your time, Chantal, and mine too, which is more important. I have many matters to attend to before handing over your estate. If you will forgive me, I should like to return to my work now."

He rose and crossed to the door which he held open for her, to signify that their interview was now ended. Linnet was speechless. It was useless to argue with this man, for he was determined not to be convinced. In the doorway she made a final effort.

"Will you do one thing for me?"

"Possibly. What is it you want?"

"Will you go to the Alhambra in London and enquire about Chantal?"

He smiled. "What should I enquire about you? How you spent your time there? Whether the stage-door Johnnies drank champagne from your slipper? How many lovers you entertained at your lodgings?"

Before she realised what she had done, Linnet's hand flew up and struck him hard across the cheek.

She stared, shocked at her own impulsive action, as he put his fingers to the slowly-reddening tinge that spread across his handsome face. Then he stood, erect and aloof, and held the door wide.

"Good day, Miss Grey." His voice held as much warmth as an iceberg. Linnet passed him, slowly and miserably, and made for the haven of her own room.

Linnet was furious with herself for her own impetuosity. What on earth had possessed her to strike the man? After all, it was not herself he was insulting, but her double, Chantal Legris. Why had she reacted so violently, when never in her life before had she offered violence to anyone? Poor Chantal. What an unhappy creature she must be if even those who knew her best disliked her so! What a pity it was that she and this man could not bring themselves to like each other enough to marry, for it would be wonderful for a poor, weak girl to have a man of such strength and integrity to rely upon. Even if Marcus Bellamy did not love his wife, she felt sure he would protect her and care for her and look after her interests well. He would make some girl a fine husband.

That thought brought Linnet back to her own problem. Somehow she must evade this marriage he was threatening. Imagine the chaos if she stayed here and was forced to go through the ceremony! Imagine Bellamy's fury when he finally discovered, as he must in the end, that he had married the wrong woman! All her efforts to convince him had failed. What was there left she could do?

Escape. There was no other way out. Matters had come to such a pass now at Willerby Manor that she must get out before she became inextricably tangled. It was a pity she could not go with Rupert when he left Willerby today, but he would almost certainly refuse to take her. He was useless as an ally. No, she would have to slip out tonight while the household slept, for then her disappearance would not be noticed until the morning.

The marshes presented a problem, but she decided that if she left overnight, she could take the time to feel her way carefully through the fields to the village, putting one foot tentatively before the other to test the surface of the ground. That way it should take no more than an hour to reach the village.

It was with some feeling of defeat that she prepared to leave, and also a feeling of guilt. After all, Cissie had disappeared in the strangest circumstances, leaving only a bloodstained shoe as a clue, and that too had disappeared equally strangely from Linnet's dressing-table. Suppose the girl was hurt or, worse still, had had an attempt made on her life. Was it not up to Linnet, as the only person who guessed or cared, to try to discover what had befallen her?

During the late afternoon Linnet heard the wheels of a carriage crunching over the gravel drive outside. She peeped out from behind her curtain and saw Rupert and Marcus, both cloaked, descend the house steps and approach the carriage. In the turmoil of her own thoughts she had almost forgotten Rupert Manning. No doubt Marcus was accompanying him to the station. She watched the coach disappear slowly down the misty drive until it was lost amid the trees.

Bellamy still had not returned when she ate dinner

alone that evening in the gloomy, candle-lit dining-room. So much the better. The less she and Bellamy had to say to each other before she left this house, the happier she would be. To try and breach that man's defences and talk to him reasonably was like trying to breach a vast, impregnable fortress alone, and equally unlikely.

And yet, she reflected as she finished her solitary meal and walked slowly along the corridor towards the vestibule, she had a strange, almost intangible feeling of regret at leaving this house. It had a desolate air, to be sure, but a wistfully sad one, as if it longed for someone to breathe life and humanity into it once again, to restore it to the vigour of its youth. Given the right inhabitants, it could be happy and joyful again. She touched the balustrade gently, tracing the moulding with her fingertips. Yes, in an odd way she would be half-sorry to leave it, despite its chill air of menace.

Mrs Price's shuffling footsteps approached from the direction of the dining-room, and Linnet turned to see her carrying a tray laden with dishes in the direction of the baize-covered door. At the same moment she caught a faint, fleeting odour of the violets again. She stiffened, then hurried abruptly forward and caught the housekeeper's arm. The woman clicked her tongue in annoyance at having her carefully-balanced tray so nearly overturned, and looked at Linnet with hostility in her eyes.

"What is the matter with you, Miss Grey?"

"Can you not smell it—violets, I swear it is."

The eyes flashed angrily. "Indeed I cannot," Mrs.

Price said, and, pushing the baize door open with her foot, she disappeared through it. Did Linnet imagine she saw a flicker of fear once again in the eyes before they looked away?

She shrugged and sighed. No matter, for tonight she would leave this house and its mysteries behind for once and for all. There was no point in concerning herself further.

As she began to mount the stairs, the front door suddenly swung open, admitting a gust of cold wind and a figure in sleet-covered cloak. It was Marcus Bellamy. As he took off his cloak and shook off the glistening droplets he caught sight of Linnet on the stairs.

"Ah, Chantal, a word with you," he said, putting his cloak aside and coming forward. Linnet hesitated on the step. "Rupert has now gone home, and tomorrow I must return to my affairs in London which I have neglected somewhat of late. So you will be alone here for a few days—apart from Mrs Price and Otto and the other servants. I hope I can trust you to be of moderately good behaviour until my return."

He turned then and strode quickly in the direction of his study. Linnet watched him go in silence. It was typical of him to make a statement thus, and not even to hint a note of query in his voice. He was not asking if she would behave well, but telling you so. Oh, how glad she would be to be rid of this domineering, unfeeling brute! With luck, this would be the last time she would ever clap eyes on the fellow!

But as she neared the top step she heard the study

door open again, and Bellamy's quick, firm tread re-enter the vestibule.

"And by the way, my dear, I forgot to add that I saw the vicar after evening service. It is all settled."

"What is settled?" Linnet's voice sounded faint and faraway even to herself.

"Why, the wedding, of course. The vicar will publish the banns at once, so the date of our wedding is fixed for one month from today."

And with that bald statement he was gone. Linnet could barely find the strength to complete the climb up the long, gloomy stairs.

SIXTEEN

Well, now the die was cast, Linnet reflected as she sat in the silence of her own room. She would have to leave Willerby Manor. She rose slowly to begin the task of gathering her own few belongings together, for she would have to replace all Chantal's clothes in the wardrobe and drawers whence she had borrowed them.

But her own clothes had been taken away, to be cleaned of all the mud and filth from the marshes! In her anxiety to be rid of this house and its strange occupants she had temporarily forgotten, but now it was essential to find them. Where would they be? In the kitchen, no doubt, but whether they would yet be dried and wearable was another matter.

Dry or not, she would have to wear them. She would take from this place nothing that was not her own, of that she was determined. Bellamy was to have no excuse to track her down again, especially as a petty thief.

Then her gaze fell on the square, white envelope on the dressing-table. She picked it up. Something bulky and heavy inside clinked as she lifted it. On the outside she read in firm, upright handwriting, "Miss Chantal

Grey. One month's allowance for November." The envelope was unsealed, so Linnet poured out its contents on to the polished surface of the dressing-table. Ten golden guineas.

Linnet sighed and began putting the gold coins back into the envelope. Then a thought struck her. She took a piece of paper and the ill-tempered pen from Chantal's desk and scratched a few words.

"I.O.U. one guinea. Linnet Grey." She wrote boldly and slipped the piece of paper into the envelope along with the money. One coin glistened still in her palm. With that borrowed guinea she could now take a train to London and her last problem was gone, save for the one of crossing the marshes at night, alone.

She crossed out Chantal's name on the envelope and wrote Bellamy's instead, then put the envelope back where she had found it. Now she had only to regain her clothes.

Linnet sat on the bed till all sounds of life at last died away in the big house. The clock on the mantel-shelf showed a little after eleven. By now the kitchen should be empty. Linnet crept downstairs noiselessly. A single lamp still glowed in the vestibule, so Bellamy must be still out of bed, probably in his study. She pushed the baize door open and slipped through.

The kitchen was deserted and the only light came from the huge open fireplace where the fire was now growing low. By its glow Linnet could discern her dress, ulster, underclothes, shoes and stockings draped over stools near the hearth. She knelt and fingered them all in turn. They were a little damp still, but no

214

longer soaking. They were wearable, if one did not much fear the risk of catching a chill. But that seemed a small enough risk compared to that of staying in Willerby Manor, subject to the whims of a man like Marcus Bellamy. In any event, she could dry them by the fire in her own room for an hour or so longer until the time came for her to leave.

She began to lay the clothes over her arm. A sudden click behind her made her start involuntarily, and she jerked round. A door leading out to the cobbled yard was opening, and a huge indistinct figure loomed in the doorway. He stopped at the sight of her crouched in the fire's glow. It was Otto.

"I am taking my clothes up to my room," Linnet stammered to explain, then stopped. What need was there for her to explain her actions to a servant, she reproached herself inwardly. It was a sign of her guilty conscience, and he would doubtless begin to suspect her intentions.

Otto's figure loomed larger in the half-light as he came forward nearer the fire. Linnet stood up and made to go, but as she did so she noticed that Otto was clutching an object in his big, work-roughened hand. It was a shoe—Cissie's shoe!

"What are you doing with that shoe?" Linnet demanded before she could stop to think. "Why have you got Cissie's shoe? Where is she?"

Otto's dark, sombre eyes regarded her soberly, but he did not answer. "Do you hear me?" Linnet insisted. His shaggy head nodded slowly. "Then answer me—where is Cissie? What have you done with her?"

The head wagged slowly from side to side, but still

215

he did not speak. Linnet was vexed by his dumb inso-
lence, but if he would not tell, then there was no way
in which she could force him. She turned to leave, to
find her way out blocked by a figure in the doorway
bearing a candle in a holder. As she held it high above
her head, Linnet could see the grizzled hair protruding from under Mrs Price's cap and a pair of puzzled
eyes watching her curiously. By now Linnet was angered and worried enough over Cissie not to fear the
woman's shrewish tongue any longer.

"If Otto will not tell me, perhaps you will, Mrs
Price. Where is Cissie, and why does Otto have her
shoe?"

"As I told you, Miss, Cissie had a slight accident,
that is all. Otto has been cleaning her shoe. But I wonder that you ask him about it, since you know he cannot speak."

"Cannot speak?" Linnet repeated. But of course,
that would account for why the creature had never
spoken in her presence.

"Why, no, Miss. Leastways, he's never spoken that
I know of. Dumb since the day the master brought
him here, though he can hear and understand every
word. Had you forgotten?"

Linnet pushed past the housekeeper and returned to
her room. The incident was of little account. She had
much to occupy her mind now, if she was to get away
tonight.

Midnight came and passed. By two o'clock her
clothes were dry enough to wear. She replaced all
Chantal's belongings exactly where she had found

them, confirmed that the gold sovereign was safe in her reticule, put on her hat and ulster, and waited and listened.

Not a sound broke the quiet, save her own subdued breathing. Somewhere out in the night a marsh bird, disturbed from its nest, chattered angrily for a moment and then settled again. Now was the time, Linnet decided, to make her bid to escape. She knew the general direction in which the village lay, and, taking time and care over her progress, she should reach it long before dawn.

By which exit should she leave? The yard door from the kitchen was the most unobtrusive way to slip out, but there was danger in reaching it. The front door presented the nearest exit, if only she could draw back the bolt soundlessly. Linnet opened the door of her room cautiously and strained her ears to listen again, then her breath caught in her throat. From somewhere far away a faint cry moaned and died, then rose again in a sobbing wail. It was from above—from the tower!

Linnet trembled on the doorstep, clutching her reticule and undecided what to do. Again the mournful cry came wavering on the night air, plaintive and beseeching. It was quite unlike the harsh and piercing scream the night Cissie had disappeared, but drawn out like a gull's mournful cry. Linnet looked about her darkened room as if in search of inspiration. Then another sound came to her waiting ears—a quick, light pattering beyond the window.

She watched the window, transfixed with fear.

217

What lay on the other side that caused the sound? As she watched she saw the light flash quickly across, bobbing as it went, just as she had seen it before.

With quick, nervous steps, she crossed the room to the window and looked down. The light was bobbing across the garden, growing fainter as it went. Linnet, still trembling, remembered Cissie's warning about the will-o'-the-wisp. But was it some supernatural thing sent to her as an omen, or was it someone's way to try and frighten her, like the peephole and the ever-present scent of violets? Did someone in this house hold such a grudge against Chantal Grey that they were trying to frighten her away before she could claim her inheritance?

Whatever it was, Linnet decided, she must leave now while she still had the opportunity. No one else seemed to have heard the wailing, for no one moved.

She braced herself to open the door and creep out. Luck was with her, and she reached the front door unmolested. To her relief, the three huge iron bolts were well oiled and slid back noiselessly, and Linnet gave no backward glance as she closed the door quickly behind her and set off down the long drive.

She could not prevent the crunch of her footsteps on the gravel, but no light appeared at any of the manor's windows. So far she had been fortunate. Pray heaven luck would continue to guide her footsteps once she reached the treacherous marshes.

The hazy silhouette of Willerby Manor quickly faded into the darkness behind her. At the far end of the drive she turned along the rutted lane that she now knew led in the direction of the church and the

village. Trees loomed up out of the dark, frightening
and full of menace in the eerie quiet, but Linnet plod-
ded resolutely on. The most hazardous part of her
journey was yet to come.

The lane was bounded on either side by a low stone
wall, and as the minutes passed, Linnet kept an eye on
the dark distance beyond the wall to the left. In that
direction lay the village, but she could see no sign of
light from an unshuttered window. It would be best,
she thought, not to venture over the fields beyond the
wall yet, until she reached the stile near the church. It
was possible the marshes here were deeper and more
dangerous.

At length she made out the shape of the church
steeple against the skyline. Now here, somewhere on
the left, would be the stile. Linnet felt along the wall
until her hands found it. Now the perilous time was
to begin. She took a deep breath and clambered on to
the stile.

For a moment she paused on top of it, straining her
eyes to peer into the murky gloom beyond, to try and
distinguish some guiding landmark which would lead
her unerringly to the sanctuary of the village. There
was nothing. Then, as Linnet began to climb down,
she fancied she caught a glimpse of something out
there. She stopped and stared again, as if concentrat-
ing could push back the enveloping velvet darkness.

Yes! There it was again, a faint glimmer of light!
Even as Linnet watched, it seemed to move and shiver
in the mist. She let go of the stile behind her and
struck out into the unknown territory of the marsh,
towards the light. Maybe it was from the village,

maybe a stranger with a lamp, or maybe even a will-o'-the-wisp, but, whatever it was, she would aim straight for it.

Linnet walked carefully, but, as before, the ground was only wet to the feet. As she progressed, however, it became soggier underfoot. The light appeared again, danced tantalisingly for a second, then was gone. Was it Linnet's imagination, or did the light seem a little brighter than before? She veered her slow footsteps towards it.

The ooze underfoot was squelching over her boots now. It would need care to cross this place. Linnet sidestepped and found firmer ground so, keeping her eyes glued in the direction of the last glimpse of light, she circled the morass and continued steadily on.

Suddenly the light appeared to rise out of the ground, brighter than ever before, dance a merry jig and drop to earth again. Linnet hastened towards it, almost forgetting in her eagerness to reach it the caution she had meant to maintain. A grassy tuft slid from under her foot, pushing it instead into a greedy, sucking pool. Linnet felt her leg give way, the icy slime slide up to her knee, clutching and pulling. She fell over on her side in the mud, fortunately firm beneath, and with effort drew her leg slowly and laboriously out of the ravening morass.

As she clambered unsteadily to her feet she saw the light appear again, and this time it could not be more than twenty yards away—a lantern, she was certain of it! Again it lurched about drunkenly, swaying to left and right and dipping unevenly as it went.

Curiosity overcame Linnet's hesitation. She stepped

out again towards the lure of the light and at once, as if it sensed her intrusion, the light dropped to the ground and lay still and unwavering. Linnet approached it cautiously, still feeling for firm ground with tentative toes.

It was an arm's length away from her. Linnet looked down, and in the pale yellow glow she could see a child's face, white and tense and wide-eyed. The eyes, dull and suspicious, stared unblinkingly back at her. Linnet felt a rush of relief. A child, some poor little thing who had lost its way from the village, no doubt—what a fool she had been to keep hearing Cissie's dire warnings about malevolent will-o'-the-wisps in her tired brain.

She leaned down to the child, putting out a hand to try to allay its fears, but at the same moment she noticed something else—the odd angle at which the head lolled, its overlarge size, and a pale flick of a tongue protruding from the corner of its mouth. A simpleton —a poor little cretin thing, no doubt rejected and cast out by superstitious villagers! Pity and anger rose inside Linnet. Poor little thing!

She murmured to the child not to fear, but the child suddenly rose to full height—a boy, no more than nine years old, she guessed—and thrust the lantern into her face. She put up her arms to protect her face and could only hear his shriek as he turned to flee. Then the shriek grew into wails, and as Linnet grew accustomed to the dark again she saw his small figure sprawled on the ground, and his arms had disappeared from sight into the ground. His legs and body were slowly sinking too, and the more he threshed about and screamed, the faster the mud began to suck him down.

"Hold still, for God's sake, keep still!" Linnet cried, and threw herself down beside him. The mud beneath her knees was luckily no more than inches deep, and she groped wildly beneath the little figure to find his armpits. In his terror the child paid no attention to her warning, and cried out and flailed madly, twisting and turning and becoming more and more relentlessly sucked in. "Lie still," Linnet cried again, but he paid no heed.

Linnet gave the little twisted face a sharp slap, and saw the mud streak across his cheek as he stared uncomprehendingly back at her. But now at least he was not struggling. She took a firm hold under his arms and leaned back, back, as far as she could go, but the devouring mud was reluctant to leave go of its victim easily. Inch by inch his shoulders appeared out of the slime, and gradually his arms came up. As soon as they were free he grabbed hold of Linnet tightly about her neck, and she felt the breath squeezed out of her throat.

"Please—not so tight—let me breathe!" she gasped, but the terrified child clung all the closer, whimpering and moaning. Still the tenacious mud would not yield up the little body, and Linnet felt the dark world about her growing darker and spinning. Her lungs, screaming with pain in their desperate search for air, felt as though they would burst, and just as Linnet fell back, with the boy's little frame still clutched close to her chest, she felt the ooze relent and regurgitate the captive child.

Thank God! Linnet lay exhausted on the ground, feeling the slime ice cold and clammy about her body, but she did not care. The little boy was safe, and whether he was a simpleton or not was of no account. He was a human creature, and the evil, treacherous marsh had been robbed of its innocent prey.

That was Linnet's last conscious thought as the blackness closed in. A pair of small arms still clung closely about her neck.

SEVENTEEN

It seemed a long, dark void before Linnet's hazy mind came to itself again, but in fact only minutes must have elapsed. The child's head burrowed against her chest, sobbing plaintively, and without conscious thought Linnet stroked the damp, mudstreaked hair and murmured soothing words to the frightened child. The lantern lay alongside them, its glass shattered and the light dead.

"Hush now, we shall be safe," Linnet said softly, struggling to sit upright in the squelching ooze, but the little body burrowed closer and clung to her like a limpet. A faint, faraway streak of light in the sky indicated approaching dawn. Ruefully, Linnet remembered her errand. She would never reach the village before daylight now.

She disentangled the little arms from her body and held the child at arms' length. His wide, tear-filled eyes stared unblinkingly at her, but his hands would not let go of hers. Poor little thing, his over-large head lolled again to one side, and occasionally his eyes rolled before they could focus on her again. She could not abandon a helpless creature in order to get to the village—she would have to see him safe before she could go on.

"Do you know the way through the marsh?" she asked him hopefully. He had seemed to know his way before she had frightened him with her sudden appearance out of the dark.

He stared back uncomprehendingly. Linnet sighed. She would just have to go on and hope. Pulling the boy to his feet, Linnet looked about for some way to rediscover the village's location. She could vaguely discern the church's indistinct steeple to the left, so the village must be this way—to the right.

"Come," she told the child. "We are soaked and very cold. We must find warmth and shelter quickly."

Cold and shivering as they both were, she put her arm about the boy's shoulders. At that very second she heard a cry, and turned to see several lights dipping and bobbing behind them. Across the watery wastes a voice came, thin and tremulous on the night air. "Miss Grey!"

A search party had come out after her, no doubt from Willerby Manor! Despair clutched Linnet. Above all else, she did not want to be taken back there! She clutched the boy tightly, determined to stride out for the village, but the child had other ideas.

At the sound of the voice he stiffened and listened, like a pointer at a shoot. Then suddenly he broke loose from Linnet's grip and stumbled off across the marsh—in the direction of the lights.

"Come back!" Linnet called. "You may fall in the marsh again!" But the child, cretin though he might be, seemed to pick his way with the unerring sense of a deer, leaping from tuft to tuft towards the voice.

"Miss Grey!" The voice was closer now, and it was undoubtedly Marcus Bellamy's. Linnet gave up, and followed the child's steps towards her captor. It was as if destiny had decreed that she was never to escape this man.

Linnet's face was set with resignation and disappointment as she reached Bellamy's tall, broad figure silhouetted against the eastern dawn. The child had run straight into his arms and was babbling some incoherent words to him. Bellamy looked up as Linnet approached, and his face showed clearly his alarm and concern.

"Thank God you're alive!" he murmured, and freeing himself from the boy he strode quickly towards her and folded his arms about her. The boy ran on to one of the other figures in the dark holding a lantern.

Linnet marvelled at the warmth and strength of Bellamy's embrace. He simply held her close, his face buried in her matted hair, and seemed completely unaware of the filth that covered him as a result. It was comforting to be held closely in strong arms thus. She shivered, partly with the icy coldness of her clothing, and partly with pure pleasure at the unexpected humanity of the man.

"You're freezing!" he commented abruptly, letting go of her. "Let us get you both back to the house quickly before you catch your death."

He drew Linnet's arm firmly through his and led

her after the others. The boy's high, excited voice squeaked unintelligible words constantly as they walked, and Linnet saw Bellamy's head nod occasionally in understanding, though he did not speak another word until they reached the manor.

The sky was lighter now as someone rang the bell at the front door. The lanterns were extinguished and figures faded away. Mrs Price appeared in her dressing-gown, flustered and agitated. At the sight of the boy's small, dishevelled and mudcovered figure she shrieked.

"Aaron, my boy, my boy!" she cried. "Whatever has happened to you?" She cast a quick, glowering glance at Linnet before gathering him up into her arms and bearing him away into the kitchen recesses beyond the baize door. Linnet watched in surprise. Bellamy smiled wanly. For the first time Linnet noticed how haggard he looked, and his eyes were reddened with sleeplessness. Had he, she wondered, stayed awake because he had anticipated her venture to escape? He turned to her and smiled again.

"I fear Mrs Price is too relieved at Aaron's safety to tend you, my dear, but I shall send the maids to fill a bath for you. See to it, Otto."

Linnet saw Otto's large frame, which she had not noticed hitherto, lumber off obediently. Bellamy was watching her thoughtfully.

"And then you must sleep, and when you are refreshed we must talk. But later, not now." He took her hand and regarded it soberly. "For now I will only say how relieved I am—no, more than that—

230

how overjoyed I am, that you are safe and well. For a while I thought—but no matter, you are safe, and that is all that matters."

A maid stood unobtrusively awaiting orders. Bellamy nodded to her to take over, and strode away. Linnet now felt too exhausted to understand or to care very much about the strange change in him. She followed the maid upstairs submissively. Her bid had ended in failure—that was all she could take in. She was back again in Willerby Manor.

Hours later Linnet awoke from a deep sleep. A figure was standing at the foot of the fourposter, watching her in silence. It was Mrs Price. For the first time the woman's face had softened from its usual harshness into a tender smile, and there was the redness of recent weeping in her eyes. Linnet sat up slowly.

As soon as the housekeeper saw that Linnet was awake, she came quickly round the bed and knelt at Linnet's side, taking her hand between both her own. She lowered her eyes and murmured, "God bless you, Miss, and forgive me."

Linnet looked blankly at her. Why should Mrs Price, who had always shown such loathing for her, now effect such concern and gratitude? The woman did not appear to notice her bewilderment, for she was muttering still.

"All these years I was wrong about you, for I did not know you had such nobleness in you. But the master told me—you saved my Aaron from the marshes, and for that I shall always be in your debt, Miss,

231

though I cannot understand it at all. But you saved him, and for that I shall do aught I can for you, always. Please forgive me."

The old woman's trembling voice was breaking with emotion. She pulled her hands away suddenly, wiped her eyes with her apron, and rushed from the room. Linnet dressed slowly, still bemused with sleep and puzzlement.

It was another of Chantal's day dresses that she put on, already laid out for her on the chair. Linnet grimaced. No doubt her own good merino was being painstakingly stripped of its layer of mud once again. The mantel clock struck twelve.

Midday already! Soon it would be time for lunch. Linnet wondered whether Marcus Bellamy would still be in the same good humour that he was when he had found her on the marshes in the early dawn, or whether by now he would have reverted to his usual laconic self. She smiled as she remembered his gentle concern. He could be devastatingly charming when he put his mind to it, this dark, saturnine Bellamy. What a pity he did not relinquish his cool reserve and appear thus more often!

Linnet left her room and began to walk along the corridor, but as she did so she heard shuffling steps and a small voice humming tunelessly behind her. She turned. There was no one in sight, but the studded door to the tower stood open. The sound came from there. Filled with curiosity, Linnet retraced her steps and went through the tower door.

Above her a small figure was toiling up the stone steps of the staircase with some difficulty. By his stiff.

movements and the odd lolling of the large head sur-
mounting a small body Linnet recognised the cretin
child from the marshes—Aaron, they had called him.
She smiled, remembering his hugging arms, and called
his name softly.

The child hesitated, then turned, his dull eyes taking
on a slow gleam of recollection and then recognition.
His gaping mouth widened into a huge grin, and he almost hurtled headlong down the steps to where she
stood. Once again his thin little arms encircled her,
and he gabbled happily into her skirts.

Linnet patted his head. "And how are you today,
little Aaron, after your soaking last night?" she en-
quired, but she suddenly lost interest in the reply
when she became aware of that scent again. Violets—
here, where she had smelt it once before in the night.
She leaned down to the child, still babbling incoherent
words to her, and realised that the odour came from
his mouth. The smell of violets was something he had
been eating.

Linnet could have laughed aloud. Sweets, of
course! The boy had been eating violet-scented
sweets, and that had been the cause of all her misgiv-
ings. How foolish she had been!

But then . . . She remembered how often she had
smelt it, not only here but in her bedroom and in the
kitchen, when Aaron had not been there. Was it indeed only the little boy who had been eating the
sweets and following her every move?

Linnet's thoughts were suddenly cut short by the
sound of a door opening above them. A woman's
figure leaned over the banister and called out, "Aaron,

Aaron!" The boy transferred his gaze slowly from one woman to the other. Linnet looked up in surprise. It was Cissie who stood looking down at them, her pale blue eyes wide in surprise. "Ah, there you are, Aaron! I wondered where you'd got to," she said.

Linnet stared. So Cissie was well and unharmed all the time! Then she noticed that the maid was leaning on a crutch and held one foot clear of the floor.

"Are you hurt, Cissie?" she asked. The memory of the bloodstained shoe rose quickly in her mind.

"Well, I was, Miss, but I'm nearly better now. I fell badly on these stairs and hurt meself—sprained me ankle and cut me foot somethink shocking, but it's nearly better. Come on, Aaron, I'm supposed to be looking after you while I'm laid up, but you gave me the slip, didn't you, little mischief? Come on now, time for lunch."

The boy let go his hold of Linnet reluctantly and climbed the rest of the stairs slowly. Cissie smiled indulgently. "Poor little thing, but he's a loveable little soul really, ain't he?" A moment later a door closed behind them both.

Linnet sighed. Really, she had been making a fool of herself, imagining a murder because of a bloodstained shoe, and dreading the scent of a child's sweets! She really must learn to curb her imagination which she had let run riot in the vast, gloomy old house.

"Miss Grey, I owe you an apology."

Linnet was brought up with a start by a tall, broad figure blocking her way at the head of the main stair-

234

case. It was Marcus Bellamy, and his face wore its usual stern expression.

"I came to look for you, to apologise. Shall we go and sit where it is more comfortable?"

He led the way to his study, holding open the door for her and treating her far more deferentially than he had ever done. Linnet took a seat in silence. Bellamy crossed to the window and looked out into the wintry sunlight that lay over the garden. For some moments he stood thus, his back to her, in silence, and then he turned.

"Miss Grey, this is very difficult for me. I am not a man accustomed to making mistakes, and therefore to apologising. But I have done you so much wrong that the least you are entitled to is my genuine apologies— and an explanation."

His tone was stiff. Linnet could see that he was embarrassed, but she did not speak. He had made life very difficult for her these last few days, and he deserved a little discomfort. He was standing by his desk now, and fingering the ink-tray disconsolately.

At length he broke the silence. "You have protested often enough that you were not Chantal, and I refused to believe you. If you were to see my ward, you would appreciate perhaps the amazing resemblance between you. But that does not excuse my stubborn disbelief. I should have guessed long ago by your demure and gracious behaviour that you were in no way like Chantal."

"I did try to tell you, Mr Bellamy."

"I know, I know. But even then I believed it was

simply Chantal's clever acting—for she is a clever actress, you know. Even the letter to the proprietress of your seminary in London could have been her clever brain-child. But I do not excuse myself. My behaviour towards you has been reprehensible and unwarrantable in the extreme, and any recompense I can make to you I shall make with pleasure."

He did not once look her in the eyes. Linnet felt glad that he was suffering for his harshness to her, but at the same time she was sorry that the warmth he had shown on bringing her home was now replaced with stiff, cold, formal politeness.

"What would you have me do, Miss Grey? I shall, of course, return you to London with all speed, and myself explain to your employer my regrettable mistake. Whether you choose to lodge a complaint with the police is for you to decide."

Linnet waited before answering and watched his set face. He was trying hard to cover his unhappiness with an expressionless look, but she could see how miserable he was. "Have no fear, Mr Bellamy," she said at length. "I have seen Chantal Legris myself and can understand how you could be mistaken. I shall make no complaint."

She watched the colour begin to return to his cheeks, and he raised his eyes now to regard her curiously. "You feel no malice towards me then?"

She shook her head. "Not now, though I confess I have done so. But I am curious to know why now, at this time, you are prepared to believe me at last. On the last occasion we met, you told me how you loathed me."

"I remember." He stroked his cheek, no doubt remembering her stinging blow.

"Then why now?"

"Because of Aaron."

"Aaron?"

He nodded, and a slow smile crept across his lips. "Yes. If you were truly Chantal, you would never have saved him from the marshes. She hated him too much. It was saving Aaron's life that finally convinced me."

EIGHTEEN

Linnet could make no sense of Bellamy's words. Why should Chantal have hated a poor simpleton boy? Superstitious folk often feared idiots, made outcasts of them even, but to hate a harmless child was ridiculous. She looked up at Bellamy enquiringly. He was gazing out of the window again, as though peering back through the mists of time.

"It was a long time ago now. Chantal was a child of but eleven or twelve and old Thomas was still alive. I was not living at Willerby then, of course, but I remember Thomas telling me of the new coachman he had hired, and how the fellow had turned out to be quite a gay Lothario amongst the maidservants, with the result that Thomas had to get rid of him quickly.

"But not soon enough, it seems. Very soon after the fellow left it became apparent that Mrs Price was distressed over something. Price is in fact her maiden name, and she was never married. Thomas soon discovered that she was to bear the coachman's child, and the poor woman was distraught. She was no longer young and had no doubt been flattered by his attentions, but now she was abandoned and dare not return to the village, where she would be ostracised for her sin."

Bellamy paused for a moment. Linnet tried hard to visualise Mrs Price ten years younger, before the grey hair and the harsh lines had robbed her of all attraction. Poor woman, no wonder she was so bitter, having been abandoned thus, helpless and pregnant.

Bellamy turned to face her. "Thomas was as kindly and concerned as he always was. He promised her she could work here, living in, and keep her child with her for as long as she wished. And when he died he asked that she should always be provided for."

"I see," Linnet murmured. "But that does not explain why Chantal should hate the child."

"I was coming to that. As you have no doubt gathered, Chantal was given to practical jokes and mischief of varying degrees of wickedness. Often her pranks were quite harmless, but unfortunately, not long before Mrs Price was to give birth, Chantal devised the idea of placing a trip-wire across the stairs. It was Mrs Price who tumbled into the trap."

Linnet gasped. What a shocking accident to befall a heavily-pregnant woman!

Bellamy clasped his hands behind his back, "I do not think Chantal realised the full extent of her misdeed at the time, but when Mrs Price went into labour and was delivered of a misshapen cretin child, she rained all her fury and disappointment on Chantal. She truly believed it was the accident which had robbed her of a perfect child and caused her to bear an idiot instead."

Linnet sighed pityingly. It was no wonder Mrs

Price had borne angry hatred against Chantal all these years.

"Mrs Price loved her child devotedly, whatever he was. But Chantal could never bear to look at him, for he reminded her of her wanton act. She hated his poor, stupid little face, and would fly into a rage of screaming hysterics whenever she chanced to see him. The result was, we had to keep the poor little thing closeted away in the West Tower, and Chantal would never venture there."

Light began to dawn for Linnet. "Then that was why the tower door was locked and I could not go there? You were still trying to keep him from my sight—when you thought I was Chantal?"

Bellamy smiled ruefully. "Yes, we tried. The difficulty was that in the two years of Chantal's absence Aaron had become accustomed to having the run of the manor, and he could not understand why he was now locked up again. He wept most bitterly."

"I heard him—in the night. And the light crossing the balcony at night—was that Aaron too?"

"Yes. His only exercise was to run in the garden at night, but never beyond it. Last night he took it into his simple mind to venture further—and it was pure luck that you saw the light and followed him. Otherwise Aaron would be dead now." Bellamy's gaze was full of warmth as he took a step towards her.

"You mistake me, sir. I was trying to escape. It was pure chance I met Aaron."

He shook his head. "Whatever the reason, the fact remains that you saved his life, and for that Mrs Price swears her undying loyalty to you. She knows now,

243

as I do, that you cannot be Chantal. Miss Grey, how can I atone to you? Tell me what you want of me, and I shall do whatever you ask."

His dark eyes were full of sorrow and penitence. Linnet felt truly sorry that a man of such strength and character should have to abase himself so. But that he had the courage to admit his mistake and apologise so graciously endeared him to her all the more. Yes, this was a man she could truly respect, this Marcus Bellamy.

"I should like to return to London, to my post, Mr Bellamy, that is all. But tomorrow, not today, if you please. There are certain things which still puzzle me and which I should like you to explain."

"Miss Grey, I should be honoured to have you as my guest for as long as you care to stay. But what is puzzling you?"

He drew a seat forward to sit by her side. Linnet felt herself colouring at his close proximity, but went on talking. "There was an odour—a scent of violets—which seemed to linger everywhere in the house. Was it Aaron's sweets?"

Bellamy laughed, a pleasant, genuine laugh. "Violets? Indeed, that is Aaron's delight. He is passionately fond of violet cachous, and those who love him often bring some for him. Especially Otto. I think Otto felt a special bond with the child, both being handicapped, as it were, for Otto is a mute. He adores the boy and plies him with cachous whenever Mrs Price's back is turned."

"So it was Otto who spied on me, then, through the peephole in my room and followed me everywhere?"

"According to my instructions," Bellamy agreed. "I wanted to be sure Chantal planned no more mischief."

"Now it begins to make sense," Linnet murmured aloud. When she had tried to question Mrs Price about the scent, the woman had been frightened because she feared Chantal was planning some mischief against her child. Suddenly everything was beginning to fit into place. Except for Cissie's disappearance the night she was to have met Linnet in the music-room.

"What happened to Cissie?" she demanded of Bellamy. "Did she truly injure her foot? If so, why was she kept hidden?"

"That is simple. Yes, she fell on the stone steps of the tower and cut her ankle quite badly. Part of her duties were to care for Aaron—who was being kept from your sight. It was simplest to keep Cissie up there with him, rather than send her home. Someone has to mind the boy while his mother sees to her housekeeping duties."

"So that is why Cissie tried to warn me away from the tower, talking of will-o'-the-wisps and the legend of the walled-up wife. She was trying to protect her charge.

"Possibly, though I believe the legend has some basis in truth. True or not, the tower has never been a particularly pleasant part of the manor, always gloomy and rather melancholy. I think Aaron will be happy to be freed from it once again."

"But the house is beautiful," Linnet retorted quickly. "It needs only fresh curtains and hangings, more lights and warmth and friendly company to bring it to life, as indeed your friend Mr Manning has said."

Bellamy nodded slowly. "You are right. But whether Chantal will agree is another matter."

Linnet felt crestfallen. Of course, the rightful heiress would have to be brought back to Willerby now the truth was known. It seemed such a pity that someone who could not appreciate its handsomeness should return to claim this place.

"What will you do now about Chantal?" she ventured timidly. "Will you go again to London to find her?"

"Yes." Bellamy rose abruptly and stood gazing into the fire. "There is very little time now before she comes of age. I must try to persuade her to come home and take over." There was no sound of pleasure in his voice. Linnet sensed that he was almost reluctant to hand over an estate he obviously cared about deeply to his ward.

"I shall go tomorrow," he said at length.

"Then, if you will permit, I shall travel to London with you."

"No." He turned quickly. "That is, if you will agree, I should like you to stay a day or two longer. I shall explain to your employer, of course, but I should like to know more about you. Tell me again about your parents."

Linnet found herself telling him once more, though this time not in angry frustration, of her sea-captain father and his doting wife who had left her at school, only to lose their lives far away. Bellamy listened attentively.

246

An abrupt knocking at the door cut short their murmured conversation. Mrs Price burst in, her usually lack-lustre eyes ashine with portentous news.

"Mr Bellamy, sir, Miss Chantal has just arrived— the real one, this time, and she's got a gentleman with her!"

Linnet rose quickly. "I shall leave you, then," she said.

"No need," a voice at the doorway drawled insolently. "I shall not disturb your intimate conversation long, Marcus."

Linnet's breath was drawn from her body in one long, admiration-filled sigh. Chantal Legris, elegant and beautiful, as poised and relaxed as a bird of paradise, stood nonchalantly framed in the doorway, half-shielding the tall, handsome young man behind her. She evidently did not see Marcus's companion clearly, for Linnet stood with her back to the window.

"I would not rob you of your all-too-seldom female company, Marcus, my dear. I came only to tell you that, as my majority is so near, I have fully made up my mind never to return to Willerby again. You may do with it as you will—I relinquish utterly my claim to the ghastly place."

She came forward as she spoke and seated herself coolly in the chair Linnet had just vacated. The young man followed her somewhat sheepishly. Linnet saw Marcus raise his eyebrows interrogatively.

"Ah, allow me," Chantal purred happily. "May I introduce Lord Percy Cherringon—my guardian, Marcus Bellamy."

247

The two men nodded in acknowledgement. Bellamy turned to Chantal again. "But may I remind you, Chantal, that Willerby is your sole source of income. Do you feel you now earn sufficiently well in your profession to be able to renounce that income?"

Chantal's laugh tinkled merrily. "My income will be secure enough, Marcus, have no fear. That is why Percy is here. He and I are affianced, and we plan to marry as soon as I come of age."

"If you have no objection, sir," the young man cut in swiftly. Marcus shrugged.

"As Chantal says, she will be of age in a matter of days now. The decision is hers entirely, without recourse to me."

"Then that is settled," Chantal said contentedly. "Percy's income is more than affluent, and he has a splendid town house in a fashionable square, which appeals to me far more than Willerby."

"And a villa in the country," Percy cut in.

"To be sure, but the town house is more to my liking, so near the fun and gaiety of London society. Now all that remains is Willerby. You may have it, if you wish, Marcus, for I know you have always cared for the place far more than I ever could. Draw up whatever legal documents are needed to see to it, and I shall sign with pleasure. You will find me at the Alhambra. Come now, Percy, there is no time to lose if I am to appear before my audience tonight."

She rose and waited for Percy to open the door. Her gaze alighted on Linnet, and she screwed up her eyes and peered closer. Linnet could see the look in

248

her wide blue eyes change from surprise to curiosity, and then to suspicion. She looked quickly at Marcus.

"What is this?" she demanded sharply. "A woman who looks like me? How did she come here? And why is she here? Is she an imposter trying to claim my inheritance?"

The frown between her eyes wrought havoc with her lovely face. Linnet made no answer. It was Marcus who had been asked to explain.

"No, Chantal. She is no imposter, and she seeks nothing that is yours. The resemblance is purely coincidental, though I grant you it is amazing."

Chantal looked puzzled still, though mollified at his reply, then instantly lost interest in Marcus and his woman friend. She took Percy's arm with a proprietary air, and he seemed very happy about it.

"Goodbye, Marcus," she called back over her shoulder, "and I wish you joy of Willerby."

"Goodbye, Chantal." And she was gone. Somehow with her going the air of oppression in the room seemed to lift, Linnet reflected. Perhaps in time Willerby would be the happier for her going, for she and the house had apparently never agreed.

Next morning Marcus had gone, promising to return by the evening. Linnet had watched from the window as he climbed into the coach, carrying his cape over his arm. He paused on the step to turn and wave, his handsome face alight with a warm smile. How elegant he was, in his frock-coat and check trousers, his high stock fastened with a pearl pin, and his top hat and gloves in his hand. What a dashing, impressive figure. Madame Roland would no doubt be highly impressed by the distinguished visitor who brought news of her errant teacher.

Willerby Manor seemed strangely desolate without his powerful presence. Linnet was content, however, knowing he would return before nightfall. She was delighted to see Cissie downstairs once again, though still hobbling with some difficulty with the aid of a stick. Mrs Price, too, kept appearing at Linnet's elbow, anxious to ensure that the young guest had all she required. Linnet was happy that now the woman's hostility was completely disappeared, and the concern she showed for Linnet proved the depth of her gratitude.

Linnet looked out of the windows at the frosted, winter white garden, seeing the small footprints on the lawn left by Aaron's happy, questing feet. He was content now, in his feeble child's mind, for he had been freed to roam as he would in the house and grounds. Linnet smiled. Already peace was beginning to creep over the old house.

She would be sorry to leave it, for all the anxiety it had caused her. It was surprising to realise that only a week ago, safe in her solitary, uneventful seminary life, she had been unaware of Willerby's existence. In so short a time the house and its occupants had played a vital role in her life, and left a mark upon her which would never be eradicated.

Linnet squared her shoulders. Soon she must leave and return to the old life, whatever feelings Willerby and Marcus Bellamy had aroused in her. So long as Madame had not yet replaced her, life would soon resume its normal, tedious routine and she must resign herself to the inevitable. In the meantime she would enjoy Bellamy's company for a few more days.

Dusk spread its evening shadows over the ivy-covered mansion at last, but still Bellamy had not returned. Linnet ate supper alone in the candle-lit dining-room, then chose to wait by the fire in Marcus's study until he returned.

She was beginning to doze off to sleep in the deep leather armchair when she heard the crunch of the carriage wheels on the drive. Moments later the study door opened. Marcus stood there, his broad, caped figure almost filling the doorway.

Linnet rose and hastened to meet him, taking his cape and laying it across a chair. Marcus sank wearily into a seat and smiled.

"Have you been waiting for me, Linnet?"

She noticed he used her own name, and it gave her infinite pleasure, spoken in such a low, caressing voice.

"I was anxious to hear your news. Did you explain to Madame Roland?"

"I did. But she was not unduly concerned. She believed you had chosen to leave, and she had appointed another teacher in your place."

"I had expected as much." Linnet could barely keep the disappointment from her voice. Where could she go now, when the time came to leave here? She sat upright, facing Bellamy, and kept her eyes lowered so that he would not see her concern.

Marcus leaned forward and sought her gaze. "There is more I would tell you, if you are not too tired."

"No, no, not at all. Please go on." She tried to

sound enthusiastic, but her mind was filled with the problem she had to face. Bellamy seemed to sense her wandering interest, for he took both her hands in his own.

"Let me tell you a bedtime story, my dear. In this house there once lived two brothers who were devoted to each other, seeking from each other the love and affection their parents did not grant them."

"Ah, yes, you spoke of them before—Thomas and his elder brother."

"Thomas and Robert. Thomas was the quieter, more studious child who idolised Robert, the gay, adventure-seeking one. He often spoke of how Robert longed to be old enough to go to sea, but his parents would not hear of it. But when Thomas was about nine years old and his brother a year or two older, tragedy struck his young life."

"I remember. Robert was killed—drowned, I believe you said."

"So it was believed, by Thomas and his parents. Robert's clothes were found neatly folded by the river bank at a point where the currents are known to be treacherous. His body was never recovered, nor any news ever discovered of him. To all the world Robert Grey was dead."

Linnet looked up at him curiously. Hearing him use her father's name caused a leap of anticipation in her breast—but no, it could not be the same. Pure coincidence, that was all.

"Until today," Marcus went on. "Today I checked all the records and registers while I was in London,

252

using the information you had given me about the date of your father's marriage and your own birth."

Linnet's heart fluttered in hope. "And the result?"

Marcus smiled. "The result was as I had half-guessed, and hoped. The strong resemblance between you and Chantal was too striking to be put down to mere coincidence. You are her cousin, both daughters of the two brothers."

Linnet could hardly believe her ears. "Are you certain? Is it proved beyond doubt?" she ventured at last.

"Indubitably. Robert's marriage certificate gave his address as Willerby Manor, for as a seafaring man he had no permanent home, other than that he had had as a boy. We can only guess that he left his clothes by the river in order to escape, to prevent his parents tracing him, so that he could run away to sea."

"But how cruel and thoughtless!" Linnet exclaimed. "To cause his parents such distress!"

"Children do not always realise when they are being cruel. To a child, one's burning ambition is all that matters," Marcus murmured. Linnet thought again of Chantal tripping Mrs Price. It was true. Children did not always realise the cruelty of their actions.

Linnet withdrew her hands from his and moved quietly about the room, trying to take in all that she had just learnt. She stopped at length and leaned over the back of Marcus's chair. "It is strange," she said, "but I have often had an odd feeling of familiarity with this house. Almost as though I knew I had some connection with it."

"A kind of inherited memory from your father, it

would seem," Marcus commented. He turned in his chair. "Are you tired, Linnet? Will you go to bed now?"

She nodded. Indeed, she was drowsy from the heat of the fire and bewildered by his news. Marcus rose and came round the chair to her.

"You see, my dear, I brought the right person back to Willerby after all," he said in a low voice, taking her hands again. Linnet looked at him enquiringly. Marcus laughed softly. "Don't you see, little Linnet, if your father was the elder son, he was the real owner of Willerby after his parents' death. And as his sole child, you are the rightful heiress now, not Chantal."

Linnet gazed at him, speechless. Marcus went on. "It will take time, of course, to prove your claim, but it is straightforward, and as Chantal has openly avowed her intention of having nothing to do with the place, there will be no litigation. It will all be resolved smoothly, and then . . ."

"And then?" Linnet repeated, too bemused to think clearly.

"Then you will be able to take up your place here as the rightful owner, and everyone will be happy."

His face was smiling broadly now, and his dark eyes sparkled. Linnet felt so safe, so secure with this strong, capable man. She looked up at him.

"But I could not manage all this—alone. Oh, Marcus, it is too much for me! I need your help!"

"I shall stay and help for as long as you want me," he assured her, and the strength of his grip over her hands was infinitely reassuring.

"Oh, Marcus, you must never leave me!" It was a

254

wonderful, terrifying thought, to be mistress of this beautiful house and estate. Together she and Marcus could bring it back to warmth and life and happiness. And she would never have to fear the lack of a home again. All her life she had wanted only a home—and affection.

Marcus was watching her. "I think Thomas would be glad to know his brother lived, and that his child would care for and love Willerby as he had done. Have no fear, I shall stay and help you as I would have done Chantal —only this time I stay happily, and of my own will."

He drew her towards the door. "I think it is time you slept now, little Linnet. There has been enough excitement for one day."

Linnet followed him contentedly, glad to be led by his strength. At the doorway a sudden thought struck her. She stopped abruptly and looked up at him.

"Oh, Marcus! The banns! You arranged for the banns to be published for your wedding! You must put a stop to them!"

Marcus smiled down. "There is time enough, little one. There is all the time in the world."

He led her along the corridors of the old house, and already Linnet fancied she could see the gloom lifting from the corners and a light beginning to flicker, enveloping Willerby in warmth and promise.